NARUTO

KAKASHI'S STORY

The Sixth Hokage

and the Failed Prince

Masashi Kishimoto
Jun Esaka

CHARACTERS

Hatake Kakashi

The Sixth Hokage. Formerly boasted the nickname "Kakashi of the Sharingan." He yielded the Hokage seat to Naruto.

Nanara

Son of the Land of Redaku's late king. Pushed out by the prime minister after the king's death, he now lives in the remote village of Nagare, far from the capital. "The failed prince."

Manari

The queen who rules the Land of Redaku, and Nanara's older sister. As ruler, she is responsible for making rain fall with a tool known as the Shuigu, but she has been unable to master it.

CONTENTS

NARUTO KAKASHI RETSUDEN
© 2019 by Masashi Kishimoto, Jun Esaka
All rights reserved.
First published in Japan in 2019 by SHUEISHA Inc., Tokyo.
English translation rights arranged by SHUEISHA Inc.

COVER + INTERIOR DESIGN Shawn Carrico
TRANSLATION Jocelyne Allen

Published by VIZ Media, LLC
P.O. Box 77010
San Francisco, CA 94107

Library of Congress Cataloging-in-Publication Data

Names: Esaka, Jun, author. | Kishimoto, Masashi, 1974- author. | Allen,
Jocelyne, 1974- translator.
Title: Naruto: Kakashi's story : the sixth hokage and the failed prince /
Jun Esaka, Kishimoto Masashi ; translation by Jocelyne Allen.
Other titles: Naruto kakashi retsuden. English
Description: San Francisco, CA : VIZ Media, 2022. | Series: Naruto |
Summary: Kakashi visits the land of Redaku in search of information
about the Sage of Six Paths, and after he finds its people miserable and
suffering a drought, he discovers a deeper plot has long been in the
works that joins his mission with Redaku's fate.
Identifiers: LCCN 2022003341 | ISBN 9781974732579 (paperback) | ISBN
9781974733521 (ebook)
Subjects: CYAC: Ninja--Fiction. | Princes--Fiction. | LCGFT: Light novels.
Classification: LCC PZ7.1.E816 Nar 2022 | DDC [Fic]--dc23
LC record available at https://lccn.loc.gov/2022003341

Printed in Canada
First printing, July 2022

viz.com

Prologue

"Ah! The top finally..."

Hatake Kakashi sighed, sick of the whole endeavor after crawling up to the peak of a mountain face that was basically a sheer cliff.

It had been twenty days since he'd left the Land of Fire. He'd been on the move day and night, and now the landscape and climate were entirely different from the country he'd left behind.

There was nothing but rough wasteland as far as the eye could see, as though the landscape had been cracked in half with a palm strike. Beyond the bleak mountains, he could see what looked like an actual town, so small it nearly vanished in the distance.

It was a long journey, but he was almost there. A couple more mountain crossings and he would at last arrive at his destination.

I wonder if they have onsens...

Judging from the harsh terrain, Kakashi knew his hope for an onsen was a futile one, but he held on to this bit of optimism as he slid down the cliff, heels digging into the face of

the mountain and sending stones clattering. The cloak he had wrapped around him flapped as he marked out a dark green trail on the deep grey slope.

He was on his way to the Land of Redaku, a city-state nestled quietly in a valley plain, hidden behind the peaks that rose up all around it. Almost completely cut off from the outside world, this country was half legend, and the countless songs sung about it stirred the imaginations of the people of the Five Great Nations.

The town was a sudden and bountiful oasis in what was otherwise the rock and sand of the mountains. Water and greenery were abundant and rich in this region throughout the four seasons, and the people lived out their days in peace and beauty, producing everything they needed as they had for centuries. In ancient times, the Sage of the Six Paths himself had favored the place and convalesced there with the beasts that were his companions. This was the version of the Land of Redaku sung about in songs.

However, the real Land of Redaku was far removed from the beatific world the poets sang of.

Was this really...that Land of Redaku?

Kakashi furrowed his brow as he entered the capital and looked around.

The town was still, as though possessed by demons. Each time the dry sandy wind kicked up, he caught the stench of dried corpses.

The area was impossibly quiet. He didn't hear even a bird chirping, much less people talking. The bodies of skinny goats were piled up haphazardly on a cart abandoned by the side of the road, but they were not the only source of the foul smell.

Long houses stood on both sides of the street, made of sun-dried bricks held together with mud, a technique characteristic

of the region. From the size of the buildings, he guessed they were private homes, but the people who should have been living in them were nowhere to be found.

Is there a famine?

He had a bad feeling as he walked toward the center of town.

This country was at an elevation of about four thousand meters, and the air was thin. His lungs hitched and his breathing grew more shallow.

He heard fabric rustling and the whistle of the wind, and his feet stopped. He turned his eyes in the direction of the sound and found a child lying on the ground beneath a now-brown aspen tree.

He raced over and picked the child up. He was first surprised by how light they were, and then by how skinny—it was like holding nothing but bones. He was further surprised at the sunken, mummy-like cheeks. The skin was oddly wrinkled, having lost its elasticity, and the burnished flesh of the cheeks looked stretched over the cheekbones, just barely sticking to the face.

Malnutrition and dehydration.

"Can you drink some water?" he asked softly, so as not to scare them.

The child raised their heavy lids from their sunken eyes. Black pupils turned slowly toward Kakashi. But even this small movement was too painful, and they soon closed their eyes again.

Kakashi took off his cloak and hung it on a branch to create some shade before kneading his chakra in the palm of his hands. With the water he created with Water Style, he moistened the child's mouth. A tongue white from malnutrition poked out from between lips to lap up the water, nearly lifeless. He had made barely enough water to fill the palm of his hand, but the child still took quite a long time to drink down even this small amount.

He sat the small body up and leaned the child against the wall of one of the houses. The child thanked him in a tiny voice and then held up the lump of cloth against their chest.

"Water for...her too...please."

Wrapped in the rough hemp cloth was the face of a baby. He gently touched the small ashen cheeks and found they were already cold.

He kneaded his chakra once more and pretended to pour the round drop of water on his fingertips into the baby's slightly parted mouth. Most of the water was absorbed by the fabric instead, but perhaps mistaking this for the baby's drinking, the child closed their eyes again, reassured.

Where were this child's parents?

He opened the door of a nearby house. The inside was neat and tidied up, no sign of any violence. He grabbed several bowls in a corner of the room, created more water to fill them, and set the full bowls next to the child.

"Sorry." His voice was thick with the word. He didn't really know himself what he was apologizing for.

The child was starving and the baby was dead.

What on earth happened in this land?

The state of the town center was even worse. Scattered corpses, nothing more than skin and bone, were covered with sand. Some were hastily wrapped in matting, others essentially exposed to the elements. The older bodies had turned black, their bellies stretched and distended, swollen with gas. The ones that were still fresh had skin dotted with blisters that seemed to have sprung up from the inside.

The only saving grace was that he saw no murdered corpses and that the dead were unlooted—their possessions remained on

them. At the very least, he knew that there had been no violence or slaughter.

He slipped past a row of long houses and had come out onto an open road when he finally found a living adult. An old woman with a bent back, carrying hay.

"Haven't seen you before," she said, before Kakashi could call out to her. "You don't live around here. Where on earth did you come from?"

"Er..." He'd come to the Land of Redaku at the request of the Seventh Hokage. The details were top secret of course, and he couldn't very well reveal his true identity to a random resident of the town. "Where do you think I came from?"

"You do ask strange questions, hm?" The old woman frowned. "Well, let's see. Your clothes are real dusty, so I'd say you came from over the mountain. You from Nagare?"

"You guessed it." Kakashi nodded, going along with the woman.

"Look at that! Got it on the first try!" She bared yellowed teeth as she laughed out loud. "No wonder you look so well. They say Nagare's got plenty of water still. Can't tell you how jealous I am."

"Where is everyone else?"

"The adults went to draw water, far off. I'm holding down the fort here since I'd only be in the way. Just to go and come back takes half a day, after all." The old woman shrugged to adjust the bale of hay on her back and then sighed heavily. "Honestly. The flooding finally ends, and now we don't have any water. A string of bad luck since the old king died."

Kakashi was stunned. "The king died?"

"You didn't know?" The old woman looked at him curiously. "Right around this time last year. Suddenly. Lots of rumors

about how he caught sick or it was something he ate, but who knows what the truth of it is."

"So who's ruling the land now?"

"His oldest daughter, Lady Manari, inherited his throne." She eyed him suspiciously. "Now I know you're from Nagare, but how could you not know that?"

"I've been ill for a long time," he said simply.

"Aah, that's terrible." The old woman smiled sympathetically.

"When did the drought start?" Kakashi asked.

The crease between the old woman's brows deepened. "I'd rather not say so, but as it happens, after Manari became queen. The rain just stopped."

The people who had gone to fetch water returned in the afternoon, bearing buckets hanging from poles stretched across their shoulders. Youths barely out of childhood carried jugs and pots in both hands.

"When was the last time it rained..." a man muttered, shrugging.

They all seemed utterly exhausted after the very long return trip.

As Kakashi helped them with their burdens, he lowered his eyes to the contents of one bucket. Fine grit and moss were mixed in with the water that had been carried from some last hope of a well far, far away, and he had serious doubts about anyone actually drinking this stuff.

"We've got no choice but to drink it. There's no other water," a tanned young woman said with a bitter smile when she saw Kakashi fish out the corpses of mosquito larva floating on the water's surface. "You said you're from Nagare? Must've been a real surprise to see the capital like this. All the water sources in the valley are drying up. There's almost nowhere left for us to get water. Just one place now, a pond in the shadows that's still holding on. But it'll dry up soon enough. And when it does, that's the end of this town."

"We could try and run away, but we got no horses," a man sighed and looked up at the sky. "If it doesn't rain soon, we're all going to die."

At this altitude, they were closer to the sky than the ocean, which was perhaps why the sky was a deep, clear blue, like a curtain had been pulled across it. Threads of clouds on the verge of disappearing slowly slipped past.

Kakashi dropped his gaze to the cracked yellow earth. Not enough water.

According to the intel he'd been given, it was the job of the royal ruler to wet the land in this dry region. The king used a tool called the Shuigu, which was handed down through generations of the royal family, to control water and make it rain.

Kakashi looked up at the stone palace rising from the center of the city. Given that this tool clearly wasn't functioning properly, the problem most likely lay there.

Eventually, when the sun's light angled off and the boundary between shadow and light grew vague, he saw a lamp light up on the top floor of the palace. Although it was still light enough outside and the birds were still happily flying around, a precious lamp had already been lit, so that was most likely the royal quarters. Much like the Hokage's office, it was in a relatively high location so that people could see where their leader was.

After waiting for the sky to deepen into a black-blue, Kakashi climbed the castle walls that were shrouded with the darkness. He peered into the lit room in question and discovered that he had been right. Standing in the center of the room was a girl in an orange gown—the symbol of the royal family. Queen Manari.

She was maybe in her mid-teens. Straight black hair hung down past her shoulders. He couldn't get a good look at her face

because her gaze was turned downward. Her hands gripped a golden staff with a ring attached to the top of it.

"So that's the Shuigu," Kakashi murmured. He'd heard of it, but this was the first time he'd seen it.

There was one other person in the room, an elderly man wearing a crimson religious robe and an ash-colored beard that reached his chest.

"Your Majesty, you must decide," the man pressed the queen, his tone firm.

Judging by the peonies embroidered in gold thread on the chest of his robe, he was probably the prime minister— the king's right hand and the most powerful person in the land outside of the royal family.

"Each day more people starve to death. It's only a matter of time until the famine reaches the outlying towns. In fact, it's already too late, but we must still devise the optimal strategy going forward."

"That's... Of course, I want to do that. But how am I supposed to..." Manari's hand trembled, and the metal decorations hanging from the Shuigu ring jangled. "I know I must use the Shuigu. But I can't muster the courage, not when I'm not sure I can control it."

"With all due respect," the prime minister said in a husky voice. "You needn't force yourself to use a tool you cannot master. If, as you fear, you lose control of it and bring about another flood, we could see more than just our crops washed away this time. If our capital is destroyed, the country will fall into a state of dysfunction."

"But...the kings of this land have used the Shuigu for centuries to wet the earth. They could do it, so I'm sure I—"

"Queen Manari." The prime minister sighed pointedly and stared hard at the girl from beneath heavy eyelids. "The records note

that those generations of kings had mastered the Shuigu from the moment they first picked it up. No one taught them how to use it—they clearly could wield it the instant they touched it. But, unfortunately, that is not the case for you."

Peering at Manari's pale face, the prime minister continued in a gentle, reassuring tone.

"This is not your fault, my queen. Most likely, some innate ability is required to handle the Shuigu, and you were simply not born with this. There is no need for you to pointlessly fixate on a tool you are not suited to. If you cannot produce water using the Shuigu, then we must simply find another way to procure the water we need."

The prime minister walked toward the window, so Kakashi pulled back. He heard the prime minister's feet stop. The other man would have been looking down on the capital from the window at the same scene Kakashi was seeing.

Tiled roofs covered in clouds of sand sinking into the sooty night shadows. Wood fires burned here and there on the roads, where people gathered to take warmth. Even on this parched earth, the citizens were desperately trying to survive. But they likely wouldn't last much longer if this drought kept up.

"Nanara hasn't tried the Shuigu yet. He might be able to use it," Manari said lifelessly from inside the room.

The prime minister snorted with laughter, still looking down at the town. "What would you have us ask that failure to do?"

"Prime Minister, that's quite rude." For the first time, Manari's voice was slightly sharp. "Nanara is my little brother and a member of the royal family. ...Even now."

"I do apologize, my Queen. My true feelings accidentally slipped out." The prime minister offered this politely insolent apology and cleared his throat before continuing. "Prince Nanara currently makes his residence in Nagare. I am told that

he hardly studies at all and instead merely plays every day. He does make things difficult. He's likely not the one who can master the Shuigu. We cannot rely on him."

Directly facing the queen, the domineering prime minister pressed her again. "Your Majesty. Your decision."

"I..." Manari fell silent and was almost frozen in place for a moment, but eventually, she squeezed out the words, "I understand. I won't use the Shuigu again. I will do as you say. I will do what I can for the sake of this land."

"Then it's settled." The prime minister nodded indulgently and clasped his aged palms together in front of his chest. "If there is no water within the country, then we will have to take it from another land. We shall go to war."

This was not a good situation.

After descending the wall with none the wiser of his eavesdropping, Kakashi leaned back against it and considered things.

He'd come this far to collect some information. But he felt that he couldn't walk away from this. The country was in ruins and the people starving because of a man-made disaster, and yet that idiot prime minister was planning to go to war with another country, of all the foolishness.

At present, he couldn't say much about Manari's inability to use the Shuigu. There was probably some condition required to activate it, like it could only be used by men or the user had to make a contract with it, as with a summoning technique. Because the previous king had died suddenly, the conditions for use might not have been correctly conveyed to her.

"Can't know anything without checking it out," Kakashi muttered to himself and looked back at the palace. The prime minister probably ruled the inside of that building with an iron

fist. It would no doubt take a while to reach the queen by disguising himself as a lady-in-waiting or a government official.

But according to the prime minister, Manari's younger brother lived in the village of Nagare. It might be a whole lot easier to approach the boy instead. The prime minister wouldn't have as many eyes that far away from the palace, and more than anything else, just hearing about this "failed prince" got him all worked up as the former jonin leading Team Seven.

The old woman he'd met that afternoon said it was about three days by horse from the capital to Nagare. On Kakashi's legs, he could likely reach it in a few hours. The issue was how to make contact.

•

The wind that was rustling the leaves of the apricot tree smelled of fresh grass.

Nanara, the eldest son of the previous king, was racing around the field with his playmate Sumure.

"Heh heh heh! Foul Sixth Hokage! Today you meet your doom!"

"Ha ha ha! Momochi Zabuza! You better apologize right now or you'll be in real trouble!"

"You're powerless before me! Here I go. Water style! Super Exploding Fabric! Pshaaaah!!"

"Hngh! If you're going to do that, then I...release Purple Lightning! Bwaaan! Craaaaash!"

They were playing Sixth Hokage. Surprised by their noisy footfalls, the grasshoppers sprang off, scattering the morning dew as they went.

"Prepare yourself, Zabuza! Earth Style! Mud Wall!" Sumure picked up a fallen tree branch and waved it around.

Nanara's face suddenly grew dark, and he glared at Sumure as though his friend had completely wrecked everything. "Come on, Sumure, be serious. Mud Wall is a defensive technique that creates a huge wall of earth! But you look like you're tossing a bunch of kunai around!"

"Oh, it is?" Sumure frowned. "Huh? What was the jutsu to summon the ninja dogs again?"

"That's the Fanged Vengeance Technique! Honestly, you don't remember anything," Nanara sighed, completely exasperated. Mud Wall and Fanged Vengeance were both super famous techniques that appeared over and over in the stories about the Sixth Hokage. So why couldn't Sumure remember them? It was so annoying.

"You just remember everything too well, Nanara," Sumure muttered. Sulking, he tossed the tree branch to the ground. "I mean, how much do you love your precious Sixth Hokage anyway?"

"Fine. I'm the Sixth Hokage now!" Nanara shouted. "Sumure, you're going down!"

"What?" the other boy cried. "I wanted to be Hokage a little longer though."

"No! It's my turn!" The words were no sooner out of his mouth than Nanara was clenching his hands into fists and charging Sumure. "Crack crack crack crack crack! Lightning Style! Lightning Blade!" He thrust a fist out at Sumure's chest.

"Whoa! Critical hiiiiit!" Sumure reeled dramatically and collapsed on the grassy field.

Nanara immediately jumped on top of him and began tickling him.

"Bwah! Ha ha! Ha ha ha ha ha ha! Stop! Stop it!" Not to be outdone, Sumure tickled Nanara in return.

The two boys shook with laugher, rolling around like rice balls on the grass.

"They've been playing at being the Hokage again since morning. Never gets old for them."

"I just know Nanara started it. He devours all those stories about the Sixth Hokage."

The villagers watched the boys as they led their goats back to the farm.

It was getting to be a year now since Nanara had come to Nagare. He used to live in the palace in the capital with his father and older sister. But after his father died suddenly and his sister inherited the throne, he came to the village.

The palace is a place of politics, inappropriate for a child. Better for Prince Nanara to grow up more leisurely in the countryside. For instance, what about the village of Nagare?

Even Nanara, a child, knew that the prime minster was politely chasing him out of the city. But that was fine by him. He had had enough of being surrounded by pompous grown-ups and locked up in the stuffy palace. Here, he had friends his age, and the grown-ups all talked to him in a friendly way, so he could forget that he was part of the royal family. He could run around in the field playing Sixth Hokage and get the adults to tell him about the legend of the Sixth Hokage. He had had so much fun every day since he came to Nagare that he could hardly stand it.

"Nanara really does love the Sixth Hokage," the villagers would say with a laugh. And Nanara would feel proud every time, sticking out his chest and grinning.

The Sixth Hokage was a legendary ninja. Ninja were these special people who could use amazing jutsu. In the Land of Fire, a place far from the Land of Redaku, super far to the east, there were supposedly a whole bunch of powerful ninja. And the

Sixth Hokage was the super charismatic leader of overwhelming amazingness that tied all those ninja together.

"The Sixth Hokage's just a fairy tale when it comes down to it." Sometimes, the villagers would say malicious things like this. "No one can actually manipulate earth and lightning. And it's not just the Sixth Hokage. I very much doubt whether the Land of Fire itself exists."

At times like this, Nanara would always reply with all the strength he had within him, "That's not true! The Sixth Hokage definitely, really, for sure does exist. He's alive right now, the ninja leader of the Land of Fire!"

"Don't be ridiculous. If ninja really exist, then how do they make lightning out of nothing?"

"They just..." He was stuck, though, when they pushed him for details.

The tale of the Sixth Hokage was a legend, so he was unclear on the specifics. The stories only ever said that Lightning Blade was lightning jutsu so powerful it could cut lightning and that it made a sound like a thousand birds. So, playing Hokage, it was important to use their imaginations to fill in the details.

Nanara knew that most of the adults thought that the Sixth Hokage was only a person in stories and didn't really exist. But...

"Um, right! The ninja are just amazing, so they can do anything! They can create lightning! Fire even! Dad said they could, so it has to be true!" Nanara would argue so sincerely and earnestly that the villagers would end up smiling and agreeing that he was right, and it must be so.

His father had taught him about the legend of the Sixth Hokage. The king of the Land of Redaku would find moments in his busy days, set Nanara on his knee, and tell him stories about the Sixth Hokage. The battle to the death with Momochi Zabuza, his fight with the evil organization Akatsuki. After

pinning his enemies up against a wall with clever maneuvering, the Sixth Hokage would lash out with the incredible Lightning Blade technique powerful enough to cut lightning. Plus, he had Fire Style and Earth Style jutsu that were just as powerful.

His father's retelling of the legend of the Hokage always got him more excited than anything else. For Nanara, the Sixth Hokage was the stuff of dreams.

"Prince Nanara, how long are you going to play exactly?"

When Margo came running after him, the hem of her skirt flapping, Nanara was in the middle of a serious contest. He had yanked up a slender Spanish needle growing in the field and was brandishing it like a sword, about to cut down Sumure who was playing the part of Zabuza.

"What, Margo? We were just at a good part."

"It's time for your studies. Come back right now!" she snapped, and Sumure's shoulders slumped. But Nanara didn't move. He was long used to Margo's shouting.

A tall woman in her mid-twenties, she lived with Nanara and took care of him. Formally, at any rate, she was a maid under direct orders from the prime minister, but Margo was different from the maids at the palace. She kept an eye on Nanara, and if he failed to finish his supper or neglected his chores, she would come flying at him with rebukes. If she discovered one of his pranks, she would give him a sharp rap on the head with her knuckles. She was more a scary aunt than a maid.

"I'm not studying today. There's no one to teach me!" Nanara stuck his chest out and announced.

He was still a member of the royal family, so the rule was he would have a tutor. The one sent from the capital by the prime min-

ister had been an incredibly quiet woman. At first, she was delighted, talking about what an honor it was to be the prince's personal tutor, but when Nanara slipped a newt down her back as a joke, she burst into tears, and the next morning, she packed her things and left. Since then, any number of tutors had come, but none of them had stayed more than two weeks. The middle-aged man who'd arrived recently had fallen into the trap Nanara dug out, broken his glasses, and stormed out of the place. That had been a week ago.

"I don't have a teacher, so I can't study. So I can just play," Nanara said, full of confidence.

Margo looked down at him with a smile. "You do though... have a new tutor."

That stupid prime minister! He already sent a new tutor?!

Nanara was quite indignant at having his fun with Sumure spoiled just when it was getting good. Well, fine. If he pulled a bit of a prank, the new teacher would certainly flee in tears.

"He's waiting in the living room," Margo said, and headed into the kitchen to make tea.

Nanara pulled off his muddy shoes and went into the living room.

There was someone on the wood stool set against the wall.

"You're late, Prince Nanara." Calm, low voice.

The someone sitting on the chair slowly turned toward him. He was backlit from the window behind him, and he couldn't really make out his face. But he could tell from the silhouette that it was a tall man. The tips of his silver hair glittered and shone dazzlingly in the light of the sun, and Nanara narrowed his eyes as if he was looking at a watchfire in an iron basket.

"You're my new tutor?" he asked, deliberately arrogant, as he crossed his arms. The beginning was crucial in all things. He

was a child, but he wouldn't allow anyone to look down on him.

The man stood up from the chair without a sound. "My name is Hatake Kakashi."

Weird name. Especially the family name.

Kakashi moved toward him, and finally, Nanara could see his face. He was a dreamy man with heavy-lidded, sleepy-looking eyes.

Chapter 1

A sloppy man. That was his first impression of his new tutor. Sleepy, goat-like eyes; messy hair. Mild, low voice, and a strangely laidback way of speaking. This would be almost *too* easy, Nanara decided at a glance.

"Hatake Kakashi?" He glared up at the man's face menacingly. "Too bad for you, I'm not interested in studying. There's only one thing I want from my tutors." He jumped onto a chair and looked up at Kakashi with shining eyes. "Tell me about the legend of the Sixth Hokage!"

"The sixth...what?"

Nanara pouted, a crease popping up on his brow. "The Sixth Hokage. You know, the hero of the Land of Fire?"

"What's that about? It's a person?" Kakashi asked in reply, cocking his head to one side.

Nanara's eyes at last grew round in surprise. "You mean, you really don't know who the Sixth Hokage is?"

"First I've heard of it." Kakashi shrugged. "This Sixth whatever, are they famous?"

"Super famous! Everybody knows who he is!" Nanara

clenched his small hands into fists and thrust his chest out proudly, as if *he* were the famous one. "The Sixth Hokage is the most powerful shinobi! *And* the greatest leader!"

"Hmm…" Kakashi's reaction was somehow lacking.

Nanara pinched his lips together. He couldn't believe that this man didn't know who *the* Sixth Hokage was. What a waste of a life! He thought everyone in the Land of Redaku had heard the legend of the Sixth Hokage at least once. And here was this ignorant fool who didn't even know his name, even though he was supposed to be a tutor.

"Well, fine." Nanara pulled himself together. "Then today, I will tell you the story of the Sixth Hokage!"

"Nah, I'm good." The rejection was quick and smooth. "Now then, let's get to your studies. That's why I'm here, after all."

"A tutor's most important duty is to tell me stories about the Sixth Hokage," Nanara sniffed.

Kakashi raised an eyebrow at this. "What did your previous tutors teach you?"

"I told you. They told me stories about the Sixth Hokage."

"Anything else?"

"And…let me play."

"Is that so?" Kakashi lowered his eyes and nodded. "It seems your tutors have been sent only for show up until now. The prime minister doesn't have any interest in making you learn anything." He stood up and gave the room a once-over. "I don't see anything along the lines of books in this house."

"Do you need books?" Nanara frowned. "They're in the library, but it's locked right now. We can't go inside. The prime minister ordered them locked about six months ago."

"He did?"

"He said it was to preserve the books. Because they'll get damaged and dirty if everyone's using them."

The library had once been open all the time, and everyone was welcome to read whatever book they wanted. But the door had remained firmly shut ever since the order to lock it came down.

"I see," Kakashi muttered, looking around the room once more. "Well, show me where it is at least."

The village of Nagare was built into the wall of a ravine. You couldn't get anywhere unless you went up or down a hill. The library stood alone at the top of the slope. The cliff rose up behind it, and a watchtower stood to one side to look out over the valley. This was the end of the village.

"See?" Nanara said. "We can't go in. It's closed."

The library was surrounded by a low hedge fence, and a chain hung between the two pillars at the front gate to prevent anyone passing through. The entrance to the building on the other side was closed tight with a brass deadbolt.

"So it would seem," Kakashi said as he stepped over the chain.

"Hey!" Nanara cried in surprise. "What are you planning to do? I mean, it's all locked up. You can't get inside!"

Kakashi walked ahead and gently touched the keyhole on the door. Then he reached for the handle and pulled the door to the side. It was supposedly locked, and yet for some reason, it clattered open.

"Kakashi! Stop!" Nanara shouted.

Kakashi looked back just as he was about to step into the library. "Hm?"

"It's illegal to go inside. Even the royal family would be punished."

"As long as no one finds out, we're all good. And if they

33

do find out, we can just apologize," Kakashi said, and stepped inside before Nanara could stop him.

Left with no other choice, the boy chased after him. He touched the front door and yanked his hand back in surprise. "Ow!"

The brass lock built into the wooden door was incredibly hot. It was almost as if the inside of the keyhole had been melted with a powerful flame. Was that why the lock had opened?

"Kakashiiii... Wait up." Nanara timidly peered inside.

It was packed with tall bookshelves. Although sunlight came in through the windows, his eyes hadn't adjusted yet, and the space was dim and gloomy. The smell of old parchment and dust filled the room.

Nanara trotted after Kakashi and grabbed the hem of his jacket.

"Where'd all that bravado from before go?" Kakashi asked, looking down at him.

"It's just..."

The decision to lock the library had been made by the prime minister. Which meant it had been his older sister Manari's decision. He felt a little guilty at disobeying her.

Kakashi let out a short sigh and then said, as if to himself, "It's important to obey rules and regulations. But it's just as important for you to read books. Well, it's basically a matter of self-discipline."

"Self...discipline? What's that?" He didn't understand the difficult word.

"It means you have the power to pull yourself up and keep going when it looks like you're going to lose at something," Kakashi said, as he turned toward the bookshelves and began picking through the books.

Standing and watching him was pretty boring, so Nanara

wandered around, kicking up dust and looking for the book he wanted. He wasn't interested in actually reading a book, but *that* book should have been in there somewhere...

"Kakashi! I found it!" Nanara held up a yellowed bound volume. "It's the Sixth Hokage book!"

"I can't believe you managed to find it," his tutor remarked.

"I can tell from the picture!" he said. The cover of any book with stories about the Sixth Hokage always had the same mark: a twisting spiral with a small triangle on the bottom left. He didn't really know what it was a picture of, but he was sure it was the Sixth Hokage's trademark.

The two of them returned to the house, loaded with several volumes Kakashi had selected and the Sixth Hokage book. They plopped down to sit cross-legged on the rug in the living room and faced each other across the low table.

"Where shall we start then, hm?" Kakashi flipped through the books he'd brought, and Nanara gasped.

What? When did this turn into a classroom?!

"Kakashi!" he shouted. "I'm not doing any studying."

"Even if we use this book?" Kakashi set the bound book with the spiral on the low table.

Instantly, Nanara relaxed. "Only if it's this book. Now, read it!"

"What are you talking about?" Kakashi replied. "*You're* going to read it. I'm going to sit and listen."

"Huh? I can't read, though. It's the tutor's job to read."

"Is it then? Well, I guess we should start with learning how to read and write."

"Hm?" Nanara cocked his head to one side, baffled. A few seconds later, he realized what Kakashi was saying, and his eyes grew round. "Learn? The characters?"

"Yes."

"All of them?!"

"Yes."

"But there are so many!"

As proof that he wasn't joking, Kakashi did not smile. He picked up a sheet of the straw paper on the table and quickly wrote a few characters on it. "This is your name. Nanara."

"Mm." Nanara propped his chin in his hands and stared at the handwriting before him, clearly set out as an example for him to follow.

"It's surprisingly simple, you know," Kakashi urged.

Reluctantly, Nanara gave in and began to copy the characters. He supposed it wasn't a bad idea to learn his own name at least. There was absolutely no way he could learn all of the characters, but he could manage somehow if it was just the two characters "na" and "ra."

He copied each one diligently, frequently referencing the characters Kakashi had written on one side of the page.

When he'd done this three times, Kakashi grabbed another piece of straw paper. "Now try to write it without looking at the example."

Brush in hand, Nanara was stumped. He'd written it three times, but he couldn't remember anything. How did the first character go again? He was pretty sure it started with a horizontal line. Wait. Was that the next character? He was getting all tangled up.

His power of concentration diminished quickly, and he turned his eyes wearily toward the window. It was really nice outside. Why did he have to be cooped up in the house on such a sunny day learning how to write...?

He started to get annoyed. He couldn't remember the "na" of Nanara at all. And why was he even doing this in the first place?

"Aaah! Whatever! We're done!" He crumpled up the straw paper in front of him and jumped to his feet. "The lesson is over!

It's way more fun to play war with everyone else. Me and Stock are the western army, Chemun and Archie are the eastern army. I'll let you be the referee."

"The eastern army and the western army?" Kakashi gazed absently at the sunlight streaming in the window. "The weather's so good today... I'm sure the eastern army will win."

"Huh?" Nanara was completely bowled over. War was a game where you split into two teams and tried to take the others' headbands. The eastern army winning just because the weather was good, it just—it totally, absolutely, definitely didn't make any sense.

"Don't say stupid stuff. Let's go!" He grabbed Kakashi's wrist and started to march away. But Kakashi didn't budge, so he ended up leaning so far forward, he nearly fell over. "Oi! What are you doing? Let's go already!"

Kakashi easily removed his wrist from Nanara's grip and let out a short sigh. "I won't force you. But reading would be better."

"Someone else will read to me, so it doesn't matter," he sniffed. "That's what the prime minister said when I was still in the capital."

"Uh-huh. Well, I'll be here, so feel free to come back if you change your mind."

Old fogey. Nanara wasn't going to change his mind. He pursed his lips together in a pout and raced out of the house.

But then he turned back and peered in through the living room window. "Kakashi's a big stupidee!" he yelled and threw his hands up.

Kakashi didn't reply or chase after him. He merely flipped the pages of a book casually, elbows on the low table.

If he's not going to play with me, then he's useless! Nanara stomped his feet angrily and ran toward the open field.

"Who was the winner?" Kakashi asked when he at last returned to the house.

"The eastern army," he replied unhappily.

"They were, huh?" Kakashi turned his eyes back to the book he was reading.

The armies had fought three times, and all three times, the eastern army had won, just like Kakashi said they would. Nanara was sure it was just a coincidence. There were only the two options: eastern army or western army. It was obvious that his random guess happened to hit the mark.

After Nanara changed out of his dirty clothes, he helped with lunch, and then devoured it. He was going horseback riding with Sumure in the afternoon now that his friend was back from grazing the animals.

"Kakashi! I'm not doing any lessons this afternoon either!" he very deliberately announced.

Kakashi finally closed his book and looked at his student. "You'd be better off giving up on horse-riding today."

He almost asked how Kakashi knew that and hurried to swallow the words. Instead, he said, "You've got no right to tell me anything!" He snapped his index finger out and then ran outside as fast as he could.

Sumure looked up from the horses in surprise when Nanara arrived. "I was waiting just in case, but I thought you wouldn't come. You have a new tutor, right?"

"I do, but that doesn't matter," Nanara replied. "I'm ignoring him."

"What's he like?" Sumure asked. "The village aunties are talking about him. They say he's tall and handsome."

"Handsome?! Not a chance!" Nanara rolled his eyes,

although he did think Kakashi was cooler than any of the adults in the village. He covered the lower half of his face with a mask, but even so, Nanara could tell he was cool. But only his face. "He's boring. He doesn't even know who the Sixth Hokage is."

"Seriously? What's the point then?"

"Yeah, no point at all."

They took the horses out to the plain southwest of the village. Straddling the saddle, Nanara kicked hard at his horse's flanks, while the falcon Ray flapped his wings to fly alongside the racing horses.

Ray was a descendant of the line of falcons that had been kept by generations of the royal family. The falcon's role was to bring the king's commands to the outlying villages, and Ray had come to Nagare with Nanara so that he could stay in contact with the palace. But no one ever sent letters, and Nanara couldn't write, so Ray was out of a job these days and flew as he wished through the skies of Nagare.

"Sumure, let's go into the woods!" Nanara shouted.

"Oh! Good idea. I got a feeling I'll find the perfect branch today!"

The pair yanked on their reins, thundered across the plains, and entered the woods. Slipping past the trees, they crossed the streams of snowmelt here and there, heading deeper into the woods. Nanara was pleased to see tiny young leaves sprouting from the treetops and sap oozing from the bark of the trunks. Spring was springing in the forest.

Sumure's horse nickered and snorted.

"So, a new foal's on the way, and my dad said I can name it whatever I want," Sumure said. "You got any good ideas, Nanara?"

"What about Pakkun? The name of the fighting dog that served the Sixth Hokage."

"It's a horse, not a dog!"

"But he shoots beams of light out of his mouth. His eyes are sharp, and he's so big he can leap over a bear in a single bound."

As they chatted about nothing important, Sumure's horse snorted once more.

"Huh?" Sumure leaned forward to peer at his horse's face. "His nose is running."

Abruptly, the horse reared up, with Sumure still on his back. He shook his head nervously from side to side and kicked anxiously before starting to buck wildly, like he was trying to throw his rider.

"O-oy?! What? What are you doing?! Stop it!" Sumure tugged on the reins, but not only did the horse not quiet, he grew increasingly agitated and whinnied loudly. Then he suddenly stopped moving before pawing repeatedly at the ground with his front hooves. With each stroke, the saddle rose up, and Sumure let go of the reins to clutch the horse's neck. It was only a matter of time before he was thrown.

"Oy! Calm down!" Nanara jumped off his horse and approached the out-of-control horse, grabbing the slender reins. "What is *wrong* with you?!"

He yanked on the reins and the bridle came right off. The buckle fastening it in place had come loose. Nanara fell onto his backside from the force of it and slammed into a stump. The out-of-control horse turned toward him and reared.

"Nanara! Watch out!" Sumure cried.

Nanara tried to roll away, but his top was caught on the stump, and he couldn't move. The thick hooves came down toward his face. He squeezed his eyes shut.

In the next instant, a powerful gust of wind slammed into his side. It was sharp and cold, like a blade, but also silken and soft somehow.

His small body was thrown up helplessly, and the collar of his jacket got caught on a tree branch. Just when he thought he'd be stuck hanging there, he slipped out of his jacket and crashed into the ground face first.

He sat up, shaking his dazed head. He didn't really understand what had just happened.

And then he saw Kakashi with his hand on the nose of the wild horse, calming it down.

"Come on, I said, calm down. Your nose is just a little itchy is all," he said, almost like he was talking to a person in the neighborhood, as he patted the horse's cheek.

Strangely, this quieted the animal, and its swinging tail finally grew still.

"Nanara! Are you okay?!" Sumure jumped down from his horse and raced over to him.

Nanara's face throbbed painfully, but thanks to the wind that had knocked him out of the way, he was basically unharmed.

"Kakashi," he said. "What are you doing here?"

"I was just out for a walk, happened to pass by." Kakashi turned toward Sumure, combing the horse's mane with his fingers. "Does this boy belong to you?"

"No." Sumure shook his head. "He's the neighbor's. Auntie Byan's."

"Is that right? Please tell her her horse has hay fever, so she should be careful in the spring," Kakashi said calmly and turned back toward Nanara. "The wind's strong today, so pollen from all kinds of plants is in the air. It's not uncommon for horses in this area to be allergic to aspen pollen."

"Hay fever? And he turned that wild?" Now that Nanara was thinking about it, he remembered that his sister had told him a long time ago that some people suddenly start sneezing in

certain seasons because of plant pollen. But he thought it was a disease just for humans, not horses.

"The reason I thought the eastern army would win was because you went out in the morning," his tutor continued. "The western army would have been facing the sun, so it would dazzle their eyes."

Bawasha. The horse gave a very sad sneeze.

Kakashi crouched down to meet Nanara's eyes and continued. "This is the sort of thing that's written in books. Studying might be boring, but it can be surprisingly useful—more than you'd think."

And so, the next day, Nanara had a brush in his hand first thing in the morning. He looked at the examples Kakashi gave him and carefully wrote each character, memorizing the shapes. Kakashi checked his work with comments like, "Don't stop there. Extend the brush stroke."

It wasn't that he'd yielded to Kakashi. Absolutely not. But now that he knew books had all kinds of things he didn't know in them, he had decided that he would get so he could read at least.

What had the wind yesterday been about? It had knocked him flying at the exact perfect moment and saved him from the rampaging horse. Almost like the jutsu of a ninja. What if the Sixth Hokage had been watching from somewhere and saved him?

"Your hand stopped," Kakashi remarked, and Nanara hurried to move the brush along the page again.

The man was flipping through books and drinking butter tea, but he was still watching to see whether Nanara was properly focused on the work. How infuriating!

"Prince Nanara, it's time to make lunch. Mr. Kakashi, would you help too?" Margo came in to say, and the lesson stopped for the time being.

Once the sun reached its highest position, the women of the village would come together and start to cook. And not just lunch. They would also make enough food for supper and breakfast the next morning. The village's communal hearth was outside, and it was dangerously dark to cook once night fell, so they made all their meals at once.

Nanara ripped up tea leaves as instructed by Margo and glanced over at Kakashi.

He was pumping air into the stove with a bellows, in charge of the fire. Nanara could tell that Margo and the women of the village were sneaking peeks at Kakashi as they peeled and chopped vegetables. He also knew that they said he was a fine man. It wasn't the whole cool thing of him wearing a mask, but maybe because his features were nicely balanced, he did look somehow like a painting standing there.

Aaah! This jerk!

Nanara tossed the tea leaves into the mixer. He added salt and butter and then turned the handle to mix it all up when Ray, who should have been on the perch in the living room, came swooping down.

"Ray!"

He flew right past Nanara and came to rest on Kakashi's arm. Kakashi tossed him some of the dried meat on the cutting board, and he deftly caught it in his beak, swallowing it down in an instant. And then as if to say "More please," he rubbed his head against Kakashi's side.

"Mr. Kakashi, please!" a woman said. "I know he's the royal hawk, but don't go giving Ray snacks!"

"Mm. He was just pestering me is all."

"Honestly! You're too nice!" the women happily teased him.

It was like Kakashi had somehow completely tamed Margo, Ray, and everyone else. He was a newcomer, but he had already made himself at home in the village. Maybe this Kakashi was someone seriously amazing. Maybe he should listen to him a little more.

Nanara turned his gaze toward Kakashi with this thought in his head and saw that the pot on the stove was boiling over. Kakashi wasn't paying it the slightest mind, focused as he was on Ray.

"Kakashi, the pot's boiling over," Nanara said, and Kakashi finally turned his face toward the stove.

"Ah!" he cried when he noticed the burbling pot. He hurriedly stood up and reached out for the now-hot handles of the iron pot with his bare hands. "Ow!" He yanked his hands back.

A few women came over, laughing, and tossed sand on the fire to get it to burn a little less hot.

"You have to watch what you're doing, Mr. Kakashi!" The amply built Auntie Byan hit him on the back, and Kakashi smiled awkwardly.

He took it back. Kakashi was too absent-minded; he couldn't count on him. And he wouldn't do what Nanara wanted! Such an annoying jerk!

I'll never fall all over Kakashi like everyone else! Nanara shouted to himself and turned the mixer handle forcefully.

His afternoon lesson was not to practice reading and writing, but actually reading a book.

"I think this book would be good."

"The tale of the Hokage is a no-go." Kakashi rejected the book Nanara held out excitedly without even a glance at the cover.

"Why?!" he cried.

"Too many difficult characters. We'll start with something simpler." Kakashi set a book with a wooden cover on the low table. When he opened it, the pages unfolded around each other and turned into a single large sheet of paper.

"Wow! A trick book!" Nanara leaned forward. The page was covered with pictures of mountains, oceans, and rivers, and dotted with a variety of characters making what he assumed were words, although he couldn't read them.

"This is a map," Kakashi told him. "It shows you which countries and villages are where and where the roads are. This one page collects all that in one place. See? These are the mountains."

"Which one's Nagare?" Nanara asked.

"It's right here." Kakashi pointed at the left edge of the map. There was just a bit of text there, all alone in the slight gap where mountain met mountain.

"So then where's the capital?"

"Around here." Kakashi pointed at the same place as before.

Nanara cocked his head to one side, baffled. "What are you talking about? That's Nagare."

"They're the same on the map."

"Huh?" He didn't get it.

"The world is incredibly large. On a map, the distance between the capital and Nagare is very small, so they're basically in the same place."

"Ha ha ha!" He didn't think the joke was very funny, but he was kind enough to laugh anyway.

However, Kakashi's face remained serious.

No, no. That was impossible.

"It takes three days to reach the capital, you know," he said finally.

"I do." Kakashi nodded. "But the world is even bigger than

you think. It would take a lot longer than that to walk from one side of the continent to the other."

Nanara stared hard at the map. If he were to believe Kakashi, the little blurred lines on the page were apparently the whole of his country.

"What about the Land of Fire? Is it on here?"

"It's right here." Kakashi pointed to the right edge of the page. The Land of Fire was apparently one of the lumps next to the ocean, silhouetted by the dividing lines drawn across the large continent.

"What? It's *that* far away?!"

Given that the scale of the map essentially erased the distance between the capital and Nagare, the distance between the Land of Redaku and the Land of Fire defied imagination.

"It's suuuuuuuuper far, huh..." Nanara propped his chin in his hands and stared at the map. "The Land of Fire is surrounded by so many countries, but the Land of Redaku is all alone up in the mountains. It's kind of...disappointing."

"You think so?"

"I mean, it's like we're hiding in a corner, living our lives, which is kind of boring, right?"

"It's pretty tough to have neighbors nearby," Kakashi said. "It leads to quarrels."

"It does?" Even as he asked this, something clicked in Nanara's head. The first time he'd been in a fistfight was after he came to this village and made a friend his own age.

"This is just my own thinking," Kakashi said as a premise before continuing. "But maybe the reason your ancestors formed their country out here was to avoid fighting. This country has been at peace all this time, right? You've never had a war?"

Indeed, as far as Nanara had heard, the Land of Redaku

had never fought with another country. Naturally. Because they didn't have anything to do with other countries to start with. For Nanara and the people of the Land of Redaku, war was something that only happened in stories in the far-off world.

"I think that was a brave choice," Kakashi said. "Avoiding fighting saves more people than winning battles."

Nanara dropped his eyes to the map. There were only large countries around the Land of Fire. The Land of Earth and the village of Kirigakure were certainly nearby.

"You think the Land of Fire is fighting lots of wars even now?" he asked.

"No. I think the danger of a war breaking out between the Land of Fire and other countries is much less than it was in the past."

"Huh?" Nanara lifted his head. "How come?"

"Because everyone knows the pain and sacrifices they will make in war are much greater than whatever they might gain," Kakashi said, looking not at the map but at Nanara. "Only a few decades ago, what was most needed to maintain peace in the Land of Fire was strength. The ninja were originally a tool to attack other countries and to protect their own country."

Nanara nodded. It was true that the ninja appearing in the legends of the Sixth Hokage were always fighting someone. Including the Hokage, of course.

"Once the major wars ended and there was some peace, the Land of Fire began actively trading with the countries around it. And then they started being able to make things. They started making one new thing after another, and their society grew rich."

"Tray-ding?" Nanara didn't know this word. He felt like he had maybe heard it from his father before. Or maybe not.

"It might not be a word that's very familiar in this land,"

Kakashi told him. "It means countries buying and selling things from and to each other. Everyone has something different that they're good at making. So, you trade what you have with someone else. That way, you can get all kinds of things."

"Ohh." *Makes sense*, Nanara muttered to himself. In Nagare, the villagers often traded things.

"If war with another land starts and trading stops, then you stop being able to get hardly anything at all, and you can't stay as rich as you were. Everyone gets poorer, and a lot of people die. If you make that sacrifice and you're lucky enough to win the war, you can force the other country to submit to you. So, what does the winner get?"

"Umm." Nanara thought for a second. "They get to feel good about winning. And be cool."

"Is that all?"

"No." He paused again. "If they chase the people in the losing country out, they can have all of their things."

Kakashi nodded. "The Land of Fire already has more than enough things, so if there was anything they'd want, it'd be land, natural resources, or technology. But they don't have to go to the trouble of starting a war for that. They can buy land, resources, and technology with money. It's much less dangerous to buy something with money than take it by force, and no one has to die. A lot of times it's cheaper than fighting."

"Uh-huh." Nanara nodded, squirming in his seat. "That's true."

"Once this way of thinking becomes almost automatic for each and every one of the people in a country, the probability of a war breaking out goes way down. Although there's economic fighting in its place."

"So then, there aren't any more ninja in the Land of Fire?"

Kakashi shook his head. "The ninja academy still exists

to teach the ninja who protect the country. And they haven't eradicated crime. Plus, some terrorist groups try to upset the balance among the nations. Still, I guess it's safe to say that the fear of a major war has basically vanished. So long as the countries' leaders don't make too huge of a blunder. Or a new group doesn't come onto the scene, filled with evil intent and in possession of power great enough to rival that of the countries." Kakashi smiled. "That's what I read in the books from the library, anyway."

Eh heh. Nanara let out the breath he'd been holding. His head was swimming after hearing so much at one time.

"There's a lot of stuff written in books, huh?"

That night, Nanara spread out the map and set it up next to his sleeping mat. Now he could look at it as he went to sleep. In the spot where the Land of Fire was, he had added a Sixth Hokage mark in bright red ink. He dove into his futon, pulling the blankets up to his nose, and stared at the spiral mark, getting excited over just that.

The legend of the Sixth Hokage went like this: "During the time of the Sixth Hokage, the Land of Fire saw unprecedented economic development and grew rapidly." In other words, the Sixth Hokage had created this world that Kakashi told him about today, where war was unlikely.

The Sixth Hokage really is amazing!

Thinking about this, he could no longer contain himself. He clutched his blanket and rolled around on the floor. He was so ridiculously happy to have learned another new thing about how amazing the Sixth Hokage was that his heart kept pounding louder and louder, and he didn't feel at all sleepy.

He sat up and stared at the map in the light of the moon.

He thought studying was boring. But maybe it was—just a little bit—fun.

More and more, he looked forward to his lessons with Kakashi with each passing day.

"I'd much rather quit all this stupid studying and go outside and play, you know!"

Although he went through the motions every morning, his voice had lost the thorniness of that first day. Studying was not very cool, and he wanted to look as annoyed and bored as he could. But his excitement for what Kakashi would teach him that day grew greater than his desire to look cool, and the corners of his mouth would sometimes curl up into a smile.

After five days of study, he could read quite a few characters. And the more he *could* read, the more he *wanted* to read. He read all kinds of books with Kakashi's help.

Kakashi taught him so many things each day. Which crops grew well in summer, which grew well in winter. He told him about ways to keep harvests from rotting, the relationships the major countries had with each other, and which things could change society in what ways. And a whole bunch of other stuff.

His tutor knew a lot of things, but there were spots where his knowledge was curiously lacking. It wasn't just the Sixth Hokage; he didn't know how to make butter tea or sugar cookies either. At times like that, Nanara would teach him. About the monarchy, about the prime minister, the queen.

Ten days passed from the day Kakashi had appeared before Nanara, and before he knew it, it was the night of the parade of the six lanterns. A custom long practiced in Nagare, six butter lamps were put onto boats made of matsubusa vines and sent down the river.

Nanara and Kakashi crouched down at the edge of the

small river that ran through the village and waited for each lamp to flow down from upstream.

"That one that went by before, how many does that make?" Kakashi asked.

"Four, I think," Nanara said. "Maybe."

It was said that misfortune would befall you if you didn't see off all of the lamps. But there was really no basis for this belief, so many villagers didn't bother to take part in the parade.

"Is there some kind of meaning in having six lanterns?" Kakashi asked, and Nanara looked at him curiously.

"It's to give thanks to the Sage of the Six Paths. You didn't know that?"

"Mm. First I've heard of it."

"Well, it's about the same as not knowing about the Sixth Hokage, I guess." Nodding, Nanara ripped up the grass at his feet, not knowing what to do with his hands. "I guess you only read hard things like maps and books about plants. You're not interested in stories."

"That's not true."

"Then what's your favorite story?"

"Hmm." Kakashi suddenly grew serious. After thinking for a while, he opened his mouth slowly. "It's hard to narrow it down to just one... But my top story'd have to be *Make-Out Paradise*."

"*Make-Out Paradise*?" Nanara frowned. "That's a weird title!"

"It's a masterpiece. Once you grow up and you can read more characters, I'll lend it to you." Kakashi sounded excited now.

Was it that good of a book?

Nanara tossed the grass toward the river and flopped down on the ground. Stars spread out across his field of view like pieces of ice scattered across the sky.

"So then what relationship does this Sage of the Six Paths have with this country?" Kakashi asked.

"There's this legend," Nanara told him. "A long time ago, we had no water. The whole country was in real trouble. There were always water shortages, especially in the area around the capital. And then the Sage of the Six Paths came along. He gave the king of the Land of Redaku this amazing tool. The Sage of the Six Paths put the power of water inside of it. But it wasn't like just anybody could come along and use it. Only the person who inherited the throne. When the king waved the tool around, rain began to fall and the whole country was wet."

Nanara noticed the fifth lantern approaching and sat up.

"Ever since, generations of kings have used the power of this tool to make the rivers swell and rain fall...I guess."

"Uh-huh." Kakashi was the one who had asked about it in the first place, but his reaction was somehow lackluster.

Nanara peered quietly at the profile of his elusive tutor. Kakashi's eyes were slowly following the vine boat floating down the river. His eyes reflected the flickering orange of the lamp, so that it looked almost like the shadow of a flame inside of a glass jewel was locked up in his pupils.

"It's just a fairy tale, though. I don't know if there actually was a Sage of the Six Paths. But the tool really exists. I saw my dad use it a bunch of times. When he waved the golden staff, it would rain."

"So now that your older sister's the queen, she uses it, right?" Kakashi asked.

"She's supposed to," Nanara agreed without hesitation.

He hadn't been back in the capital once since he came to Nagare. But he was sure she was carrying out her official duties wonderfully. Because she was his serious and smart big sister, and he was proud of her.

Chapter 2

A letter arrived from the palace for Nanara. The anniversary of the previous king's death was upon them, and Nanara was to come to the capital.

"I'm not going," Nanara announced and shut himself in his room.

There wasn't a lock on the door though, so Kakashi could have opened it if he'd wanted to. Instead, he knocked and said, "How about you come out and we go pick your horse? You need to leave tomorrow if you're going to make it in time."

"I don't want to go to the capital."

It was just a brief trip back to the palace where he'd been born and raised, so he should have been happy, and yet, for some reason, Nanara was stubbornly against it.

Kakashi looked at Margo. "Is it always like this?"

"Couldn't say." Margo shook her head. "This is the first time a message has ever come from the palace."

Kakashi knocked on the wooden door again. "An order from the palace is official. You might be a prince, but you can't ignore it."

A mumbled reply came finally from the other side of the door. "What'll happen if I do?"

"There'll be punishment. For Margo."

Margo was his official guardian. If Nanara didn't go to the palace, he would be in defiance of the queen, and Margo would be the first to get the whip.

Nanara waited a bit and then opened the door ever so slightly. Peeking a timid face out, he looked at Kakashi and Margo in turn as he muttered, "I'll go to the palace."

Margo's relief was fleeting.

"But," Nanara added, pushing his head out further through the crack in the door. "You come too, Kakashi. Then I'll go."

Farm work needed to get done that wouldn't if three horses were taken from the village, so Margo ended up staying in Nagare.

It was a three days' ride from Nagare to the capital, including changing horses along the way.

Kakashi and Nanara rode alongside each other and stopped at a town along the way before night fell. Nanara didn't reveal his royal status, but even so, the townspeople welcomed them and offered them a meal and comfortable lodgings for the night. Naturally, this wasn't free. Nanara paid for this hospitality with the jewels that Margo had made Nanara bring along. There were no inns or anything like, so Nanara and Kakashi slept separately at whatever houses had an extra futon.

That night, Nanara tossed and turned in his bed. He couldn't get to sleep.

He should have been exhausted from being on horseback since morning, but he couldn't sleep. He felt gloomy and sad, a heavy rock in the pit of his stomach thinking they would be at the capital in two more days.

He finally gave up on sleep and got up. It was the middle of the night, but fortunately, a full moon hung in the sky, and it was light enough to see even without a lantern.

He was wandering about when he noticed the light of a butter lamp swinging beneath the wisteria trellis in the plaza.

Kakashi.

He was sitting on a rock in place of a chair, the spine of a book set on a propped-up knee, reading. Wisteria blossoms spilling from the vines fluttered in the breeze, alternately hiding and revealing him.

Kakashi noticed Nanara and slapped the book closed, casually covering the front of it with his long fingers. "What's the matter?"

"Nothing. I couldn't sleep, so I was just taking a walk," Nanara muttered sulkily and turned around, but he stopped when Kakashi called out to him.

"If you can't sleep, why don't you read for a while? One of those stories about that Sixth Hokage you love."

"If I read something like that, I'll be even more awake."

"So then practice your characters," Kakashi said, walking over to him.

"I...would probably fall asleep pretty quick," he admitted.

The scent of wisteria flowers that trailed after Kakashi was cold and sweet like frozen honey, and mixed with the light of the moon, it dizzied him somehow.

Nanara awkwardly let out the breath he'd been holding. He knew the reason why he couldn't sleep.

"Kakashi. I...don't want to go to the capital."

"Is it because there's someone you'd rather not see?"

Nanara kicked the ground and nodded reluctantly. He was honestly annoyed that Kakashi hit the mark so easily, but for now, his desire to talk to someone outweighed his irritation.

"Is there someone there you're scared of?" Kakashi asked gently.

Nanara frowned and said nothing.

"The prime minister?"

"I don't want to see him either, but...it's mostly my sister," he said and clamped his mouth shut.

Kakashi waited for a bit to give Nanara the space to continue, but he stayed quiet. He stayed where he was though, right by Kakashi's side.

"I've wondered about this for a while," Kakashi started slowly. "Why did your sister inherit the throne and not you? According to the customs of this land, the first in the line of succession is the eldest son."

Nanara stared at the ground. "'Cause my sister's way smarter than me."

"Is that all?"

"I..." He looked up at the butter lamp in Kakashi's hand. The chilled, strained night air softened a little around the lamp, rocked by the flame. "I didn't want to do it."

He clenched his small hands into fists.

"The prime minister asked me if I would succeed the throne...and I said that I wasn't going to, so my sister should."

"Why?" Kakashi asked.

"Why?" Nanara repeated. "Because it'd be boring. I hate studying... There's no way I want to be stuck at a desk working from morning till night."

Like my father, he added in his head. He should have had so many fun memories, but the only look on his father's face he could remember now was a frown. Apart from when he would sometimes play with Nanara, he was always holed up in his office.

"Anyway, the prime minister said he'd respect my wishes. So my sister ended up inheriting the throne."

"Was that something she wanted?" Kakashi said.

"I don't know." He shrugged. "But she said she would do it. And then the prime minister suggested I move out here, so I ended up living in the village, far away from all the politics stuff."

"Do you regret that choice?"

Nanara shook his head lifelessly. "Living in Nagare is super fun. But...maybe I shouldn't have done that to my sister."

He had known that his kind sister would take the throne in his place. That was exactly why he felt all right about walking away from his right to inherit. He'd been certain that his sister would never be as irresponsible as he was.

And everything had gone just as he'd expected. Manari accepted the throne and Nanara obtained his freedom.

"I pushed everything onto her. I took advantage of her kindness."

"So that's why you're afraid to go to the capital."

Nanara hesitated for a second and then nodded. "I'm scared to see her. It'd be okay if she was having fun being queen. But... if she's not..."

"If she wants to quit being ruler?" Kakashi casually spoke the words that Nanara had avoided and looked him straight in the eye. "Would you take her place and become king?"

He didn't want to. But he also didn't want to cause his sister pain.

Nanara pursed his lips and dropped his eyes. Kakashi's shadow fell onto the dry earth, stretching out in a strange shape. And what popped into Nanara's head was his father's face.

"I won't be king," he said quietly.

"Nobody's going to force you to." Kakashi's voice grew even kinder. "But you might change your mind after you get to the capital and talk with your sister."

Kakashi put his hands on Nanara's shoulders and whirled

him around. He could see the house where he was staying ahead on the road he'd come down.

"You should probably get back to bed already. Tomorrow we'll be sleeping outside."

Nanara nodded and started walking but then stopped and looked back. "You'll come with me all the way to the capital, right, Kakashi?"

"Of course. I am your tutor, after all."

Kakashi waited until Nanara was out of sight before again opening the book he'd been reading.

The legend of the Sixth Hokage.

He supposed that someone at some point—and no doubt mostly for their own amusement—had collected into a book all the stories and rumors that got passed among merchants. This volume had then made it all the way to the Land of Redaku and unexpectedly taken root.

If they were going to turn someone into a myth, I wish they'd picked a hero who's a little more heroic, he thought. His own personal recommendation was the Fourth. He admitted that it was hard to pass over the Seventh, but Naruto's story wasn't complete yet, so there was no point in starting to tell it now.

"Never thought I'd see the day when I could read a book based on my own self," he muttered, stroking the dark paper of the cover. Nanara wouldn't stop going on about his precious Sixth, so Kakashi had grown curious despite himself and picked up the book to see what all the fuss was about. Having read it now, he had to laugh at this ridiculously glorified fictional version of himself.

In the book, the Sixth Hokage was always a hero. Equipped with both strength and kindness, he was levelheaded and never

upset, always working to pull people forward. There wasn't a word about him being awkward or pathetic. Nothing of his inability to save his cherished friend or the fact that his only reason to continue fighting was to try and make that up to this friend.

He nearly sighed at the enormous gap between fiction and reality, but he supposed legends were like that. Only the stories that shine, episodes that linger in the mind, are selected, transformed, and passed on, becoming increasingly detached from the truth.

It had been the same with his father, a man with such power that the Three Great Shinobi paled in comparison—the "White Fang of Konoha," half-revered as a living legend by other lands. But the real man had been the sort of person found in any village anywhere. He'd had his stern side and his troubles, and the words of other people could hurt him just like anyone else.

Kakashi wasn't even ten years old when he served as chief mourner at his father's wake. It had been a sweltering summer night. The air had been so hot and humid, he'd had trouble breathing. He remembered very well feeling almost like he'd been locked up underground.

Kakashi had been the first person to discover the body of Hatake Sakumo after he passed and left his son behind, and it had also been Kakashi who reported this death to the Hokage at the time. Having had a long career as a jonin, Sakumo was fairly well known, and many people attended his wake. But not one of them truly mourned him. At least, it appeared so to Kakashi.

"He was so strong, and yet gone so soon."

"First, he breaks the code, then suicide? How irresponsible."

"His dad's dead, and the kid's cool as can be. It's a bit creepy."

"Of course he died, a guy like that."

The whispered voices reached Kakashi's ears whether he liked it or not. He sat formally on his knees at the far end of the room, patiently waiting for the line of visitors to sprinkle incense at the altar and go.

"It's like I killed you, ain't it?" a man spat at the memorial picture of his father. The friend Sakumo had disobeyed the rules to save. "I never asked you to, y'know. So not only do you up and quit the mission, you kill yourself? What a sorry excuse of a man."

Kakashi held his tongue.

Many people came to speak their own selfish words to the dead. Kakashi felt like he would lose his mind if he tried to consider which of them was right and what was true.

The clear thing was that his father had died because he disobeyed the rules. If he had followed the rules and left his comrades to die, he would have still been alive.

There were far fewer people at the funeral the next day. Apparently, most everyone had been satisfied with briefly gossiping before his father's photo at the wake.

The short ceremony ended, and Kakashi walked home alone. Perhaps a little drunk on all the sutra-chanting, the world wobbled before him, and he felt ill. Both his mind and his body were clumsy, not quite working properly. Darkness fell in his field of view, and the noisy chorus of the cicadas faded away. But even the simple act of stopping was too much of an annoyance to him. Nothing mattered anymore.

His feet tangled beneath him and he pitched forward. Into someone's back.

"You were really strong back there," a voice told him, and he suddenly saw bright golden hair.

He felt his breathing become a little easier.

The Yellow Flash of Konoha. Namikaze Minato.

"You can just stay like that on my back," Minato said, but Kakashi immediately pulled away to stand on his own two feet.

Minato was famous in the village, well known as a shrewd ninja and thought to be next in line for Hokage. Kakashi had spoken with him a number of times, but they weren't particularly close.

"Excuse me. I haven't been sleeping, and I tripped over my feet," he said, politely formal, and started to bow and be on his way, but Minato grabbed his arm.

"Kakashi, Sakumo was—"

"My father broke the rules and died," Kakashi forceful-ly interrupted Minato and then continued dispassionately. "Obeying the rules and our codes is only natural for a ninja. My father didn't have the conviction to follow through. Even though emotions do nothing but get in the way."

It was only natural that Kakashi was in pain given that his father had just died, but even the awareness of this ordinary emotion had scared him back then. With no one to blame for these feelings, Kakashi had become stubbornly fixated on obey-ing the rules.

A few years later, Minato became Kakashi's boss and teamed up with him, Rin, and Obito in a four-man cell. It was then that Kakashi learned that the rules were not everything, and that sometimes, there were things he should put ahead of the rules. Thanks to Minato, Kakashi grew to accept the father he hadn't been able to acknowledge.

Minato and Obito had affirmed the father that he rejected. And he felt like he'd only been able to lift the lid on his feelings for his father and face them for the first time after these two comrades acknowledged the dead man. And then they had died too, and Kakashi was wracked with grief with each of their deaths. But it was also their presence in his life that had hauled

him back up onto his feet again. Now he felt proud from the bottom of his heart to have been born the child of the White Fang of Konoha.

•

Nanara and Kakashi continued to plod along on their horses. It was the morning of the third day of the journey since they departed Nagare.

Just half a day away from the capital, two messengers from the palace were waiting for them on the road.

"The prime minister sent us. It would be terrible if you were to lose your way," they explained.

This was strange. Now that they'd come this far, the path led straight to the capital. But the messengers walked ahead to deliberately lead them on the clear road and took a detour to enter the capital not on the east side, which was closest to the village of Nagare, but on the north side.

The main road from the northern gate to the palace was the center of the capital, with large houses crammed along either side. Booths were set up along the way, selling the country's specialties of salt, saké, and silk, and business was booming. The people coming and going all worked for noble families or the palace and were well dressed, no dirt on their faces like the people of Nagare. When they saw Nanara, they stepped aside and made a path for him.

"The capital's still as busy as ever, hm?" Nanara said, looking around from on top of his horse. He had meant his words for Kakashi next to him, but Kakashi didn't reply. Maybe he didn't hear him.

They tied their horses to a hitching post and entered the palace. They had no sooner stepped into the corridor inside than the queen was coming out to welcome them personally.

"I'm glad to see you, Nanara."

"Manari..."

In stark contrast to Nanara's hesitant step backward, Manari raced toward him happily and peered at his face.

"Have you been well? What's life like in Nagare?"

Her voice was the same as it always was, and the tension finally left his shoulders. What a relief. His sister was smiling.

"I have a ton of fun every day," he told her. "You look good too. I'm so glad."

"Now listen. I wanted to give you this." Manari took something from her sleeve and pressed it into Nanara's hand. "It's yours. A memento of father. Because you didn't choose a keepsake."

A blue gem cut into a hexagon hung from the end of a silver chain.

"Don't tell the prime minister, okay?" she said. "It's valuable, so I'm not supposed to give it away without following procedures and getting permission."

"Thanks, Manari!" Nanara hung the chain around his neck and hid the gem beneath his shirt.

"Don't lose it."

"I won't. I promise."

"Prince Nanara, you must be more polite when speaking to the queen."

Manari's face clouded over the instant they heard this low voice echo in the corridor.

The prime minister marched toward them, the hem of his long robe dragging showily behind him. Grey beard, husky voice. He always spoke in an overly polite manner to Nanara, to the point where it seemed almost malicious.

The prime minister glanced at Kakashi. "And who is this?"

"My new tutor," Nanara told him. "The last one quit."

Although it was supposedly the prime minister who had dispatched Kakashi, this was at best in name only. In actuality, lower-ranking officials just picked tutors as they saw fit. So Kakashi was meeting the prime minister for the first time that day, and he'd asked Nanara in advance to please introduce him.

"Is that so? Well, well." The prime minister stared hard at Kakashi, and then shifted his gaze to Nanara. "It is the custom on the first anniversary of a death for the royal family and the senior government officials to have a noon meal together. I have no doubt you are quite exhausted, so please, take some time to rest in your room before we meet. A maid will come for you once the preparations are complete."

"Oh. Okay." Nanara glanced back at Kakashi. If possible, he wanted him at the dinner.

Meeting his eyes, Kakashi guessed Nanara's feelings and shook his head. "I'm sure an outsider like myself would only be in the way at a dinner like that. I'll stay in my room."

"You will..." Nanara's face fell. "Prime minister, prepare a room for Kakashi."

"For this man?" The prime minister was clearly vexed as he looked Kakashi up and down. "Those who are not of the royal family or government officials are not permitted to stay in the palace. I will arrange lodgings for him elsewhere."

"No," Nanara said curtly. "If Kakashi's not here, I won't stay in the palace either."

Kakashi shrugged exaggeratedly. "Could you make it a room with a big window? I don't do well in the damp."

The prime minister sighed. "Take him," he reluctantly ordered a maid waiting by the wall.

They're late.

Nanara waited impatiently in his own room for dinner to be ready. Even though it was clearly past noon, the prime minister still hadn't sent anyone for him.

"Prince Nanara, your dinner is ready," said the maid who finally came for him, and he frowned at her odd wording.

It all fell into place for him, however, when he entered the dining hall. The adults had finished eating and were pouring each other glasses of post-dinner apricot liqueur. They had taken care of all the inconvenient discussions before the child arrived.

"That took forever!" Nanara gave full voice to his displeasure as he pulled out a chair. He sat up as straight as he could so that he could rest his elbows on the round table, which was too tall for a child, and looked around at the adults.

The prime minister next to the queen haughtily ferried rich goat cheese into his mouth. Senior officials A, B, and C pretended to listen carefully to the prime minister's pointless chatter, fawning smiles on their faces. And Queen Manari focused her gaze on the wood grain of the oak table, as though she was trying desperately not to meet anyone else's eyes.

"I did in fact have another reason for calling you to the palace, Prince Nanara," the prime minister began without waiting for Nanara's dinner to be set before him. "We will be dispatching the army to Nagare. Over the next few weeks, some fifty soldiers will stay there for approximately ten days. I would ask that you make the preparations to provide rations for them during that period."

"Huh?" Nanara blinked a couple times, unable to understand what the minister was talking about.

"Um, we're starting a war," Manari added ever-so-timidly. "The capital has a serious water shortage. So we're invading a rich country to get a new source of water."

Nanara looked back and forth between his sister and the prime minister, baffled. Soldiers? Invade? What on earth were they talking about?

"Manari," he said. "Explain this to me."

"It is perhaps somewhat difficult for you to understand, Prince Nanara," the prime minister said.

"Then explain it until I do," he commanded in a hard voice.

"Is that your wish?" The prime minister leaned back against his chair, annoyed. "Where to begin then... Our land has a relatively harsh environment, compared with other countries. Summers are hot, winters are cold, and the majority of the land is poor with an overwhelming lack of natural resources. If there is a famine, no one will come to help us. We've just barely managed to eke out a life sowing wheat, but we will never see any real development. And thus, it has been decided that we shall move. To a richer place. We will go to war, steal new land, and live there."

"New land?" Nanara asked. "Where exactly are you planning for us to live?"

"The Land of Fire," the prime minister replied immediately.

"Huh?" Nanara lifted his face in surprise. "The Land of Fire?"

The prime minister nodded. "A few years ago, at the discretion of the previous king, I descended the mountain. I travelled east from the Land of Redaku over several months and toured the outside countries. After I passed through the mountains and crossed several countries, I found the Land of Fire did indeed exist. The ruler there is not called a king, but rather a daimyo."

The senior officials apparently hadn't heard the Land of Fire part, and they all looked at each other with confusion. This was the first time in the history of the Land of Redaku that the existence of the Land of Fire had been officially confirmed.

"So then," Nanara started. "Was the Sixth Hokage there?"

"Yes, he does in fact exist. Unfortunately, he was out of the country for a conference, so I was not granted an audience with him. What surprised me was the development of the Land of Fire. The country was richer than we could even imagine. Plenty of food, excellent medical and welfare systems. Using highly developed technologies, they make lumps of metal dozens of kilometers long move at incredible speeds. The people get in these lumps and are transported around the country. And everyone has devices small enough to fit into the palm of a hand, which they use to share information dispatched from far-off places. No one dies of starvation there. In fact, many people die from the intake of too much sugar."

"I don't...really understand," Nanara said nervously, putting a damper on the prime minister's excitement. "You're saying that you're planning to go to war because you want us to be like the Land of Fire?"

"That is exactly correct. The Land of Fire has not experienced war in over a decade. We could say in fact that now, when they are drunk on peace, is precisely the time for an attack." The prime minister smiled, liver-spotted cheeks twisting upward. "Prince Nanara. You do know that in the Land of Fire and the neighboring countries, there are fighting groups called 'shinobi,' yes?"

Nanara nodded. The shinobi were amazing people, who kneaded chakra to generate fire and water from nothing. The unparalleled Sixth Hokage was also a shinobi.

"While I travelled to those neighboring countries and studied the manufacturing processes for heavy firearms, I forged connections with some powerful shinobi. Shinobi who left their organizations and now act independently—the so-called 'rogue shinobi.' For our war, I have hired fifty of these rogue shinobi."

"Fifty...shinobi..." To Nanara, shinobi were like gods. He

thought of them as different creatures, like mountain rabbits or snow leopards. He couldn't immediately digest the idea of hiring fifty such creatures.

"But," one of the officials said hesitantly. "It won't be that easy to get to the Land of Fire from here."

"The ninja will move us in twenty days a distance that would take half a year by horse cart," the prime minister responded with a smirk.

The mood in the room clearly began to change. Fifty of these "shinobi" would be their allies. Thinking about it like this, the senior officials started to feel like they had a chance at victory. That was how special the shinobi were to the residents of the Land of Redaku and its total lack of offensive power. It was no wonder that their faces began to shine with expectation.

"The water shortage this year is a trial given to us by God," the prime minister said. "When we overcome it and secure new land, our country will develop. Just as the Land of Fire did."

Nanara turned his eyes to the untouched meal that sat before him. Yak cheese the color of the sun. Flat noodles made with flour and beans, turnip and wild vegetable miso soup. Salted goat meat, butter tea. And plenty of apricots. He ate things very similar in the village of Nagare, although there were fewer dishes there.

All of it was food that could be gotten in this country. If they started trading with other countries like Kakashi said, would they get many more kinds of food on their tables? Having never left the country, Nanara couldn't imagine what other kinds of foods there were in the world.

But what was wrong with the way things were now? To Nanara, what lay before his eyes was indeed a feast. He had never even thought about wanting to eat other things.

What had the prime minister seen outside the country?

Was the food out there really that good? Was it worth taking, even if it meant war?

Nanara looked at his sister. "You agree with this, Manari?"

"Yes." She nodded, but her eyes remained fixed on her empty plate, as though some kind of answer was written there.

"We have already received the consent of her Majesty," the prime minister said. He stood up, came around to Nanara, and leaned forward. "In a mere decade or two, the Land of Fire accomplished astonishing technological development. This is courtesy of the might of the Sixth Hokage. However, during the era of war and unrest, I hear that even he spent all his time fighting as a shinobi. Prince Nanara, if you truly do aspire to be like the Sixth Hokage...then would you not give the people of our country the same experience as that very Sixth Hokage?"

Yellowed eyes bore through him, and Nanara nodded vaguely, before popping one of the apricots on his plate into his mouth as if trying to get out of this conversation.

•

The room the prime minister had selected for Kakashi was plenty humid, as if to spite him. There was only one small window to let in light, so even though it was high noon, it was quite gloomy.

"Master Kakashi. I brought tea."

"Thanks. Could you just put it there?" he asked.

The maid stepped toward the wooden chest he indicated with his eyes.

Thuk.

He struck her very lightly with a hand strike to the back of the neck. She lost consciousness, staggering forward, and Kakashi caught her with one arm. She would have felt no pain at all. She had simply fallen asleep.

The sleep chakra point, a technique he had learned directly

from Iruka, the principal of the ninja academy. When Kakashi mentioned in conversation that he had trouble sleeping sometimes, Iruka had taught him a secret jutsu for inducing restful sleep. The sticking point, though, was that it was hard to hit the spot on yourself, given that the chakra point was on the back of the neck.

Kakashi laid the softly snoring maid on the bed and wove a sign.

The art of transformation!

Bompf! Smoke rose up, and Kakashi was now a perfect copy of the sleeping maid. His plan was to change his appearance so that he wouldn't catch anyone's eye and could move openly around the palace.

Transformed into the maid, he tucked the wooden tray under his arm and left the room. With a very ladylike gait, he walked quietly down the long hallway.

He wanted to investigate two things. One was the Shuigu handed down in the royal family. The other was the period when the Sage of Six Paths had stayed in this region. He had come to this country to begin with to look into the Sage of Six Paths for Naruto.

Information gathered where people gathered. The laundry room, the kitchen, or...

"Oh! Hey! You! New girl!" someone called out, and Kakashi stopped. Was he the new girl?

Two maids beckoned him from inside of a nearby room. One had a broom, the other a dustpan. They appeared to be in the middle of cleaning.

Kakashi stepped inside, and they leaned in close.

"You brought Prince Nanara's tutor tea, right?" one asked.

"What's he like?" said the other.

"Er." Why were they curious about a mere guest like

Kakashi? They couldn't have found out he was a ninja from Konoha, could they? Kakashi reflexively braced himself, hyper aware of the position of the knife beneath his skirt.

The maids continued, eyes glittering.

"Where did they find such a sullen tutor, hm!"

"Right? I'm really into that kind of downer-ish old guy."

"Uh-huh," Kakashi said idiotically.

The maids kept chatting, getting more and more worked up, without realizing that the man in question was standing before them.

"Hiding his face, though. That's a mean trick!"

"I wonder if he's married?"

He didn't really understand what was going on, but that was fine as long as they didn't suspect him. He casually let his gaze roam over the two women. One of them was the boss, judging by her outfit. One pocket of her long dress bulged out in the shape of a key ring.

"Um," he hesitantly interjected, playing the new girl. "It seems like there are a lot of rooms. Are there many visitors coming to the palace?"

"Been a lot lately. Look, see there?" The maid went over to the window and pointed outside.

A number of white yurts were set up on the plain that stretched out to the east of the capital.

"The prime minister just hired a bunch of army people, and that's their camp. Even though there's a water shortage and we can't grow anything here, we have to provide rations for all of them. It's terrible."

"And I guess he's paying them *very* handsomely," the other woman noted. "The prime minister says those people are going to solve the water shortage."

Ninja. Everything fell into place for Kakashi when he saw

the movements of the people coming and going among the tents. From the size of the camp and the number of tents, there were maybe fifty of them. The prime minister had hired ninja to go to war with the Land of Fire.

"Water! Too much, too little, trouble either way," one of the maids complained. "Six months ago, you know, there was this huge flash flood and all the fields around here got washed away. I guess the flow of snowmelt changed because of a landslide up near the top of the mountain. Or at least that's what the prime minister said."

The flood had most likely happened because Manari couldn't control the Shuigu. But it seemed like the maids didn't even know such a tool existed.

"Things are getting bad." The other maid clucked her tongue. "Only a matter of time before the food stores are empty. But we work at the palace, so we'll manage somehow."

"Everything's been upside down since Queen Manari took the throne. I miss the old king."

Finding his chance to jump into the conversation, Kakashi changed the subject. "I never actually saw the old king. I only moved to the capital recently."

"There's a portrait of him in his office. Aaah, but we're not allowed to go in there."

"We're not?" Kakashi said. "I'll have to be careful not to go in by mistake. Er, where was it again?"

"Third floor, end of the hall."

The new maid smiled and thanked her kind colleagues before leaving the room.

Kakashi walked calmly down the hallway, turned the corner, and went left at the landing on the stairs before pulling out the bundle of keys caught on the tip of his kunai. He had quietly pinched them from the pocket of the boss maid.

After checking there was no one around, he unlocked the double doors and slipped inside.

The room was silent. All four walls were covered in bookshelves that reached the ceiling. This was the former king's office.

The books were shelved seemingly at random, and their spines formed a kind of mosaic. Among stacks of volumes on the history of the Land of Redaku, anatomy, pictorial guides to plants, and *The Collected Legends of the Sixth Hokage*, Kakashi found one without a title on its spine and reached out his hand. It was at the very edge of the very top shelf, a position that his middle finger just barely reached with the maid's height.

The discolored straw paper was held shut with silkworm thread. A skilled hand had written "Manuscript: Six Paths Journal" on the dyed wood cover.

Found it.

The record of the Sage of Six Paths' sojourn in this nation. Unfortunately, however, only the cover was written in modern language. The text inside was not in the common language, and he couldn't read a word of it. Still, the book was an important find.

He tucked the manuscript away in his top and continued peering at the shelves. From what he'd gleaned from the maids' conversation, the people in the palace were not aware of the existence of the Shuigu. There was a good possibility that the former king hid *that* in his own office.

If my guess is right, if I can find it, the capital's water shortage will be over...

He looked up and noticed a familiar spine. He'd seen the same red leather book on a lower shelf. Why would there be two copies of the same book?

He picked it up and found that it was in fact a book-shaped case. Inside was...a letter.

"What are you doing?"

"Prime Minister." Kakashi returned the book to the shelf and tweaked the face of his transformation jutsu before turning around. If he were seen in the study wearing the maid's face, that girl would get in trouble. "Excuse me. It's gotten quite dusty in here. I was going to clean up a bit."

"The previous king's office is an administrative area. No one is allowed to enter without permission," the prime minister said sharply and walked over to Kakashi, the heels of his wooden shoes clacking against the floor. "What of the tutor that Prince Nanara clings to?"

"He's resting in his room."

"He is? Anything suspicious about him?"

"No. I didn't notice anything in particular."

"I see." He took another step and stopped immediately in front of Kakashi.

"Sir?"

"Oh. The tutor I hired for Prince Nanara was a young woman, you see." The prime minister's tone was oddly familiar, considering that he was speaking with a strange maid. "And then at some point, that man became his tutor. Who hired him, I wonder?"

"I have no idea, sir. Perhaps the adults of the village simply assigned a suitable person?" the maid answered, and the prime minister yanked on her arm. "Eeek!"

The force of the prime minister's hand was too much for her slender frame, and she quickly lost her balance. Kakashi

thrust a hand out against the wall to act as though he were just barely staying on his feet.

The prime minister peered at his face. "Apparently, those shinobi can transform themselves into the spitting image of another person. You be careful not to get replaced without your knowing it."

"Yes sir. I heard that Master Kakashi is just a regular tutor, though." Kakashi swung the bob that reached his shoulders and cocked his head to one side, playing innocent.

"One more thing." The corners of the prime minister's mouth curled up. "A few weeks ago, someone somewhere filled the cistern with fresh water. Thanks to that kind soul, we haven't had a single famine death since. You wouldn't happen to have any thoughts on who could've done such a thing and how?"

"Oh my!" The maid opened her eyes wide in surprise. "Are people dying of famine outside of the palace?"

The prime minister stared very carefully at her face and her gestures, clucked his tongue, and turned on his heel.

Aah, yikes. Bad. That prime minister is as distrustful as he looks.

Once Kakashi was back in his room and had released the transformation, he tapped on the shoulder of the real maid, asleep on his bed with her mouth open.

Her eyelids fluttered and then lifted, and in the next instant, she leaped up with a gasp. "I-I-I-I am so sorry! I can't *believe* me! Falling asleep in a guest's room!"

"You must be tired. Well, it's no wonder. Here. Thanks so much for the tea." He downed the now ice-cold tea in a single gulp and held out the empty teacup.

The maid walked toward the door, fixing her hair as she did so, and Kakashi called out to her as though he had just

remembered something. "Oh, actually! Could you take a look at this book?"

It was the manuscript on the Sage of Six Paths that he'd nicked from the king's office.

"I borrowed this from the prime minister, but I can't read it. The characters are pretty different from what we use in the Land of Redaku these days."

"Ohh. That's an ancient script," the maid replied, peering at the page. "This is the language they spoke in this area ages ago. No one uses it now. I heard there's no way to decode it anymore."

"So I guess there's no one who can read it?"

"I don't suppose there is," she agreed. "There's talk of getting rid of those old books since it's pointless to save them when no one can read them."

Either way, he'd better send the book to the Land of Fire as soon as possible.

Kakashi waited for the maid to leave and then turned to the window and gave a signal. The hawk waiting on standby came gliding down. He tossed the manuscript, and the bird caught it deftly in its sharp claws. It wheeled around, spread its wings, and flew off into the eastern sky, almost gliding. To the Seventh Hokage of Konohagakure.

At best, it would arrive in two days. He'd written a note about how he'd found it and the situation here and slipped it inside the book. It was too bad that the manuscript was written in an ancient language, but he was sure that Sakura or Shikamaru would be able to decipher it.

He was watching the hawk grow smaller in the sky when Nanara knocked on his door. The boy looked glum and was holding a book to his chest.

"How was the dinner?" Kakashi asked.

Nanara didn't reply, but instead thrust the book out at him, lips still tightly pursed. "Read this."

He was about to tell Nanara to read it himself. Why else had Kakashi put all that time into teaching him the characters? But then he stopped.

"All right," he said. He eased himself into a chair and opened the book, and Nanara dropped down to sit on the rug.

Of course, the book Nanara had brought was *The Legend of the Sixth Hokage*. This one had a different cover than the volume in Nagare.

Kakashi didn't turn the page. Instead, he kept his eyes on Nanara. "Are your sister and the prime minister maybe wanting to go to war?"

Nanara looked stunned. "How did you know?"

"The maids were gossiping about it."

Nanara picked at the rug and stared at the characters that read *The Legend of the Sixth Hokage* on the cover of the book. "The prime minister said we're going to war with the Land of Fire. What do you think, Kakashi?"

Even if you do, you can't win. But Kakashi couldn't say that yet, and so he asked a question instead. "What do *you* think about it?"

Nanara thought for a minute.

"I think what the prime minister really wants to do is trade. He wants to have relationships with other countries and get rich. But there aren't any countries around us, so he wants to go to war and take some land," he said slowly, while also looking up at Kakashi questioningly. "You said before the Land of Fire started trading lots once they were at peace, right? But this country's always been at peace. So why's he want to take from another country now?"

"Maybe because this isn't peace."

"Huh?"

Kakashi stood up and looked out the window. The sun was just starting to set. "How about we go outside for a minute?"

The Land of Redaku was over four thousand meters above sea level, and the temperature plummeted when night drew near.

Kakashi came out on the south side of the palace with Nanara in tow, the opposite side from the northern district with all the noble houses. This was where the common people lived.

"There's kind of a strange smell," Nanara said. "Is something rotting?"

"Something is probably rotting," Kakashi agreed.

Nanara opened his mouth to ask what and then froze.

Bodies were piled up one on top of the other on woven mats spread out on the street. Sooty hair spread out beneath the stomachs of people lying face down. They had been left there for quite some time already; the bodies were turning black in places and emitting a terrible stench.

"Huh..." Something pushed up from inside his stomach. He reflexively crouched down, but since he had barely eaten at the dinner, all that came up were gastric juice and some undigested butter.

Why.

Why are these people here dead.

"Kakashi, let's go." Deathly pale, he tugged on his tutor's sleeve, but Kakashi gave Nanara a push, forcing him to step forward.

"This is your country," he told him.

"No..." Nanara replied lifelessly and wiped the corners of his mouth. He was part of the royal family, but he wasn't king. This was his sister's country. "Kakashi, did you know this was happening in the city?"

"I heard about it from the maids," he replied. "They said with the water shortage and the crop failure, people were dying."

I didn't know about any of this. Wait. Water shortage? Isn't Manari using the tool?

They kept walking and came out onto a plaza. Nanara was on edge, wondering what miserable scene they would encounter, so he was a tiny bit relieved when he saw the people gathered in the plaza.

They had set scraps of wood on fire here and there and were huddled together around them, taking warmth from the flames. As they chatted, one person or another would smile every so often. But they were, without exception, emaciated, with limbs that were nothing more than bones with skin stretched over them.

Now he understood why Kakashi had told him to change into the clothes he'd worn from Nagare before they left the palace. If he had come out here still dressed for the dinner, the embroidered orange gown and jeweled hat would have been torn from his body.

"Stay right here. I'll be back before you can count to a hundred."

Kakashi's words basically went into one ear and out the other.

A pigeon had landed in the square, and the look in everyone's eyes changed immediately. One man tried to sneak up on it. But the bird took a few steps, head bobbing and weaving, and then it flapped its wings and set off into the sky.

The plaza was blanketed in dejection. Everyone was hungry.

"What's that scared look for? You want some?" A thin man noticed Nanara and pulled a wooden skewer from the fire, offering it to him. A lizard hung on it, twisted up in an S, its back sliced open.

Nanara paled and shook his head. It was repulsive. How could *that* be food? He took a step away, and his back hit a wall

on the edge of the plaza. The strength drained out of his legs at last, and he slumped down on the spot.

He couldn't believe the capital had come to this. There was no way his sister and the prime minister didn't know what was happening. They had decided on war precisely because they did know about it. Everyone was thirsty and hungry. This country needed water and food.

If they fought, would they be able to get what everyone wanted?

Nanara looked around the plaza again.

He saw a little girl peel off some bark and suck on it. Her chest and stomach were so sunken he almost wondered if something was wrong with his eyes. She was only about half as wide as a child of the same height in Nagare.

Nanara reached into his shirt and grabbed the gem against his chest, the precious keepsake of his father that his sister had given him earlier. He was sure he wasn't the one who needed this gem.

He approached the girl and put the jewel in her hand. She looked up at him with wide eyes.

"There's still plenty of water in the north district. If you trade this for money, they'll sell you some." That was all he said before he raced away from the spot.

A small gesture like that wouldn't really make things better, but it had to have been better than doing nothing. Would his father have praised him if he'd seen it?

He ran along without really looking where he was going and slammed into someone. Kakashi.

"Let's go home." Nanara tugged on Kakashi's sleeve. "I get it."

On the way back to the palace, they could see faint wisps of smoke rising up to the east of the capital.

"The shinobi the prime minister hired are camped over there,"

Kakashi said, his eyes lingering on the base of the smoke. "The maids were saying that rations are distributed to them first."

Nanara lifted his gaze. It was dusk only moments ago, but the sky was dark in the blink of an eye, and now the grey of the smoke melted into the mostly navy sky.

"He hired fifty shinobi," he whispered, dropping his eyes to the ground. "You think maybe even the great Sixth Hokage'd fall up against that many shinobi?"

"Instant death, I expect," Kakashi replied.

"For whom?"

"The fifty nobodies, of course. A random group of average shinobi doesn't begin to compare with the Hokage. Plus, there are plenty of strong shinobi in the Land of Fire besides the Hokage."

When the man standing guard at the palace gate saw Nanara and Kakashi outside, the look on his face revealed he would be in trouble. They'd slipped out of the palace without anyone knowing, and this guard had probably been told not to let them outside. They ignored him and went inside.

"The Land of Redaku can't win against the Land of Fire. But even setting that aside, what the country should be doing now isn't war," Kakashi said coolly. "A country develops faster and better by building friendly relationships instead of fighting other countries. The history of the Land of Fire is proof of that."

"The problems would be solved if there was water, so why—" Nanara started to say and then snapped his mouth shut because a maid was walking toward them.

"Master Kakashi, perfect timing." It was the maid who had shown him to his room that afternoon. "I have a message from the prime minister. He wishes for you to attend to Prince Nanara and come with him to breakfast tomorrow."

•

Kakashi pulled on his jacket as he entered the dining hall the following morning, where everyone else was already seated.

"Oh, I'm late..."

At the table were Nanara, the prime minister, and the queen. An unlikely group for lively conversation. He sat down in an empty chair, and a maid silently laid breakfast out for him.

"I heard that you will be leaving this afternoon. If only you could have a more leisurely stay." The prime minister's comments hung in the air. But chit-chatting about travel plans was not the reason he'd made sure that Kakashi was seated at the same table as the queen. Not when the prime minister had been so reluctant to even let Kakashi stay within the walls of the palace.

Kakashi scooped up some jam with a wooden spoon.

How far did the prime minister have his hooks in Manari? Were they thick as thieves, or was she simply being forced to go along with him? He wanted to dig into this, but she wouldn't meet his eyes. Or anyone else's for that matter.

"That reminds me," the prime minister said. "It seems that you went for a walk in the southern district with Prince Nanara last night."

Here we go. The main event.

The jam was sweeter than he'd expected, and Kakashi frowned at the taste as he nodded. "I did."

"You must have been surprised at the current drought we're experiencing. It's been causing us no end of worry."

"Seems best to deal with it quickly, don't you think?" Kakashi said. "If it keeps up, a lot more people will suffer, I expect."

"The truth is, three weeks ago, someone replenished the

reserve cistern in a single night. Thanks to that act, we haven't had a single death recently." The prime minister's gaze was probing as he continued. "As of yesterday, the cistern had dropped by two-thirds. But this morning, it was full again. I wonder who performed such magic for us. You wouldn't happen to know?"

"No." Kakashi thought for a minute and shook his head. "It's the first I've heard of anyone dying from starvation. But perhaps it would be best to try and fix that? Just because the cistern went and filled itself twice doesn't mean there'll be a third time."

"Yes," the prime minister agreed. "That is why we go to war. Have you already had a look at the group of shinobi I've hired?"

"Sister," Nanara suddenly called out to Manari.

It was only her little brother, and yet Manari stiffened. "What?" She lifted her face awkwardly.

"Why don't you use the Shuigu?"

The expressions on the faces of Manari and the prime minister changed instantly. The maids noticed the way the air in the room had frozen, and they looked at each other dubiously.

In this charged atmosphere, Kakashi alone retained his cool, as though no one had said anything of any importance. He ignored the others and spooned rice porridge into his mouth.

"If you use the Shuigu like Father did, you can fix the water shortage," Nanara insisted. "Why don't you do that?"

"You will be quiet," the prime minister said in a low voice, glaring at Nanara. "The existence of the Shuigu is confidential. We may be inside the palace, but this is not a topic for light conversation."

"Can't you use it?" Nanara asked.

The color drained from Minari's face.

The prime minister clucked his tongue before slamming his goblet down on the table. "You left the palace. That is none of your concern. Queen Manari is genuinely troubled by the matter of the Shuigu. It is not your place to speak of it."

"Troubled?" Nanara said. "You mean she can't use it? She can't use the Shuigu, so there's not enough water. That's why you're going to go to war and take it from other countries?"

The prime minister slowly exhaled and glared at Kakashi, a blue vein popping up on his forehead. "Was it you who whispered these things in Prince Nanara's ears?"

"Hm? I don't know what you mean." Kakashi cocked his head to one side, confused. "I don't even know what this Shuigu you're talking about is."

Perhaps because of everything that had transpired over breakfast, when Kakashi and Nanara left the palace later that day, neither the prime minister nor the queen came to see them off.

They walked through the residential area on the south side, leading their horses, rather than taking the main road of the north. There had been a fair number of people around when they visited in the evening, but the area was deserted during the day. They caught glimpses of a few children, and that was it. The adults had likely gone to fetch water from somewhere.

Nanara averted his eyes from the corpses on the road and kept his head down the whole time.

The bodies were all emaciated, and exacerbated by the dry climate, many dried out and became mummies before they rotted. Even so, maggots crawled around mouths and nostrils, and the buzzing of flies followed them like the sound of rain at a distance.

The surviving residents were no doubt at a loss for how to deal with the bodies. In the Land of Redaku, burial was the mainstream, but a significant amount of work was required to go and bury a person outside of the capital.

When people die, they get heavier.

Kakashi knew in his bones the weight of the recovered bodies of comrades, the weight of colleagues who died while still on his back being carried to safety, the weight of the single eye given in the final moments of a close friend who he didn't even get the chance to carry on his back.

He didn't want to do any of that ever again. That was exactly why Kakashi had pushed the development of Konohagakure as the Sixth Hokage. Many, many people had criticized him, saying he was disrespecting the old traditions. But he never wanted to repeat the days of war again.

A never-ending peace. *That* was what Kakashi had sought as the Sixth Hokage. An orderly society that would go on and on even when he was not the Hokage, even when the day came when the role of Hokage disappeared. To create a framework so that they would never again fall into the quagmire of war.

This was the sole tribute the survivor Kakashi could offer to his dead friend. Because that friend had told him to become Hokage. He had been desperate to get as close as he could to realizing the world without absurdity that his friend had thirsted for.

For a long time, Obito was the reason why Kakashi continued to fight. And now he was the needle on the compass Kakashi used to guide him on his path forward. His reunion with Obito, Rin, and his master was no doubt still far in the future, but he very much wanted to live in a manner that he could be proud of when they did finally meet.

Which was exactly why he couldn't turn his eyes away from what was happening right before him, this whole situation in the Land of Redaku. And Naruto and his difficult predicament in the Land of Fire.

"Sir," someone called out, and when he lowered his gaze, he saw a skinny girl standing there. It was the girl Kakashi had met

on his first day in the Land of Redaku. "You're the one who gave me water that time, right?"

Kakashi said nothing and pushed back the hair plastered to the girl's face. On her right cheek was a reddish-black bruise, exactly the size of an adult fist. Her small nose was broken, twisted, and the blood that ran from her nostrils to below her chin was completely dried. Clearly marks from someone hitting her.

The girl pushed the wooden bowl she held in both hands toward Kakashi. "Give me more water."

Kakashi crouched down, held his left hand over the bowl, and poured water into it. As he did that, he touched the girl's cheek with his other hand and let chakra flow into it. He wasn't particularly versed in medical ninjutsu, but he could at least ease the pain.

"What happened to your face?" Nanara's trembling voice came from behind Kakashi. "What happened to the jewel?"

"Jewel?" Kakashi frowned.

Nanara ran over and grabbed her shoulders. "Who did this to you?!"

Shocked, the girl shrank back. The wooden bowl fell from her hands and spilled onto the ground. For a second, she stared at it, but then ran off and left it.

"That girl," Nanara murmured, watching her go. "Why didn't anything change? I gave her the jewel, but...why?"

"What?"

Gave her the jewel?

Nanara rambled on plaintively. "I gave it to her. A necklace with a big jewel on it, a keepsake of my father. It was blue and beautiful, and she should have been able to buy lots to eat at least if she traded it for money. So why is she still looking for water? Why... Doesn't she know how to trade for money? But then the adults in her life would...help..."

He cut himself off abruptly, realizing what he had done. What would happen in a country with so many starving people if he gave just one of them a gem? Especially if that one of them was a small, powerless child.

He let out a silent cry and began to shake. Kakashi placed a hand on his trembling shoulders, and Nanara squeezed Kakashi's bony fingers, clinging to them.

Chapter 3

The hooves hit the rough ochre of the well-trod road from the capital to Nagare at regular intervals.

Nanara was silent, his eyes focused on the backs of his hands. He held the reins so tightly, they rubbed painfully against his hands, and blood welled up on his palms.

"Who hit her?" Nanara muttered.

Kakashi looked at him. "Do you think whoever hit the girl is to blame?"

He shook his head. Whoever hit her and took the jewel was no doubt also dying of thirst. The fault lay with his own ignorant self in giving the girl the jewel in the first place. And with the palace leaders who had created a situation in which a person would hit a child out of a need for water.

To get that water, the prime minister and Manari were planning to go to war with the Land of Fire. Fifty shinobi would stay in Nagare for ten days. Nanara would have to start preparing as soon as they returned to the village if he was going to have the rations the prime minister requested ready in time.

"Kakashi, how much wheat do you think we need to feed fifty shinobi for ten days?"

"Hmm, good question."

The number that Kakashi gave was much bigger than anything Nanara had imagined.

•

They stopped for the night at the same village they had along the way and reached Nagare past noon two days later.

The villagers were just harvesting the wheat they'd sown in the winter. It was the men's job to take scythes to the tawny stalks. The children then took up great armfuls of the harvest and carried it to their mothers. The mothers sat in a circle in the shade and deftly separated wheat from chaff. The final step of exposing the wheat to the wind to blow off the remaining bits of chaff was, for some reason, the work of unmarried women.

"Prince Nanara, you're back, hm? And you too, Mister Kakashi. Welcome home!" Margo called out in a cheery voice from the ridge in the field. She hoisted her full basket up to tickle the sky and set it on her head, bits of chaff catching in the wind and fluttering down.

Nanara loved this sight.

It was the day when they gave thanks for the blessings they received from nature and gathered up the year's food. But the majority of the wheat harvested now would be given up to an army for war.

"Everyone, listen to me," he called out to the villagers, as he climbed up onto the stones piled up to divide the fields.

"Nanara. Welcome back! How was your sister?"

"Master Kakashi, welcome back from your long journey."

The villagers gathered around, sweating, faces covered in dirt, as they brushed away the chaff on their clothes.

Nanara looked out at them, his face hard. "You don't have to carry the harvested wheat to the storehouse."

"Huh? Why not?" Sumure cocked his head dubiously to one side, a bundle of wheat in his arms.

"The queen's army will soon be coming from the capital," Nanara said. "We were asked to prepare rations for their stay here."

The villagers' faces began to cloud over at the ominous sound of the word *army*.

"And how many people would that be?" someone called.

Nanara glanced back to look at Kakashi, watching over the proceedings.

"Fifty people. They'll be staying for ten days or so," Kakashi replied on Nanara's behalf.

The villagers were stunned into silence. Fifty people was a third of the population of Nagare. To have that many people stay for ten days was, to put it bluntly, a burden.

"The prime minister said we have to," Nanara explained, staring at the ground as if to avoid critical eyes. "We have no choice. They're going to war."

"War?! Where?" Eyes wide as saucers, Margo immediately followed up with more questions. "With whom? Why?"

Nanara lowered his eyes even further and said in a vanishingly small voice, "With the Land of Fire. He said they want richer land."

The villagers looked at each other.

"So the Land of Fire really exists."

"But it's incredibly far away. How will they get there?"

"An army? When did we get an army? There wasn't one during the king's reign."

In all of its recorded history, the Land of Redaku had never fought a war. None of the villagers could even imagine what combat with another country would look like.

"You said they're going to war seeking water. Does that mean there's not enough water in the capital?" Margo asked.

Nanara was stuck for a minute.

"Everything's fine. Nothing's changed, not yet." His voice felt unsteady as it spun this lie. "But the water source will dry up in a few years, so the prime minister says that we have to get ahead of that and get some other land."

"Why?" Margo persisted. "Is the prime minister's army so strong they could win against the Land of Fire?"

"Margo. You can't go asking Nanara that. He won't know," one of the villagers said, with no malice. "If the prime minister's decided to go to war, all we can do is obey his orders."

"But..." Margo looked even more worried, but most of the villagers already had some measure of resignation on their faces.

"We did all the work to harvest this, and now it's going to be taken from us," Sumure said dejectedly, staring down at the wheat piled up in his basket.

•

"Nanara, are you really reading that?"

"...I'm reading it," he responded listlessly and dropped his gaze back to the *Illustrated Guide to Mushrooms in the Four Seasons* that lay open on the table. He couldn't concentrate at all on the lessons he normally enjoyed so much. It might have been important to learn how to distinguish between mushrooms you can eat and mushrooms that can be medicine, but he had problems more pressing than mushrooms right now.

The queen's army was coming. But he still couldn't figure out what he should do.

The prime minister said they could get water if they went to war. If that was true, then he should offer the wheat to the coming army and support them however he could.

But...would this country really become wealthy if he did that?

Kakashi said a group of rogue shinobi couldn't win against the ninja of Konoha under the Hokage leadership. If that was true, then starting a war was a mistake.

"Unh." Nanara flopped forward onto the mushroom guide. Everything was all tangled up in his head.

Everyone was saying something different. Who on earth was he supposed to believe?

What popped up in the back of his mind was the little girl's swollen, reddish-black face. He never wanted to see anything like that again. That much he knew. But what exactly was the right thing to do to keep it from happening again?

"All I have are problems since you became my tutor." Nanara looked up at Kakashi resentfully. He only meant to complain a little, but once he started, he couldn't stop. His unhappiness just spilled out of him. "It was way easier when I didn't know any hard stuff and I could play Hokage with Sumure every day. Now because you taught me all this, I understand all kinds of things, and I'm thinking all these things, all the time, just round and round."

"I suppose you would." Kakashi nodded. "Well, that's what it's like to know things. If you want to protect the people around you, your only choice is to become strong. You have to have a spirit strong enough to lead everyone."

"I'm not the king. I don't need to lead anything," Nanara retorted, as the face of the beaten girl flashed through his mind again. He felt guilty, but his mouth wouldn't stop. "I'm not smart like you. I don't know anything. Don't think I can do everything the way you can."

In contrast with Nanara's increasingly wild tone, Kakashi was the picture of calm. "I'm not as capable as you think I am. If that's how I look to you, it's probably thanks to the fact that I've been blessed with the people around me. In my masters,

my colleagues, my students... I honestly don't deserve all the blessings I have."

Well, I'm blessed, too, he thought, but the words didn't come out of his mouth. Instead, he slammed the book full of mushrooms shut. "Kakashi, what should I do?"

"You have to decide that yourself or it's meaningless."

Kakashi only ever said things that weren't truly answers. He was really struggling here, and Kakashi wouldn't help him even a little.

"If we don't obey my sister and the prime minister, I'm sure they'll attack Nagare," he said. "But if I obey them and go along with the war, a lot of people will die."

"But if no one does anything," Kakashi countered, "everyone will die because of the water shortage."

That was exactly it.

"I hate all those things. I can't choose."

"You have other choices. You could stop the prime minister's army with force."

"Don't be ridiculous!" Nanara lost his temper and leaped to his feet. "It's fifty shinobi! There's no way I could beat them... So everyone should just die?!"

He knew he was just ranting, but he couldn't keep from shouting. He knew in his head that Kakashi hadn't meant it like that, but he still couldn't stop. Emotion welled up from deep inside, and his heart pounded. The fact that Kakashi could sit there so calmly made him even angrier.

"I'm sure if you act justly, there's a path where no one has to die," his tutor told him.

"I can't choose it," Nanara said through clenched teeth and flew out of the room.

That night.

Unable to sleep, Kakashi stared at the low ceiling.

Not wanting to choose either option—he understood Nanara's feelings painfully well. As the Sixth Hokage, he had been presented with options he didn't want to choose many times.

He absolutely couldn't say he'd made the best choice every time. He had no doubt that more than one person hated him so much, they would have happily murdered him.

When he had paid a courtesy call to the Land of Waves as Hokage, in amongst the crowd welcoming him with cheers, there had been an old lady who spat at him. In tears, she shouted accusingly that her son had been killed by a Konoha ninja. The war might have been over, but so many still lived with wounds that could not heal.

In this world, there were people who viewed the Konoha ninja as heroes and those who held deep animosity toward them, and as the Sixth Hokage, Kakashi had been a target for both. It was the Hokage who bore the brunt of all these emotions, showered in the respect and contempt of an unknown number of people. As leader, he'd made a lot of hard decisions.

Now was no different. If Nanara knew who Kakashi really was, he would likely reproach him and ask why he wasn't helping in a more direct manner. After all, it wasn't like Kakashi couldn't knock fifty or a hundred average ninja flying if he set his mind to it. Plus, if he kept producing water with his jutsu, he could solve the water shortage for as long his strength held up.

But there wouldn't be any point in that. The people of this country had to learn how to stand up and walk under their own strength.

Give a starving person bread or teach them how to grow wheat. As Hokage, Kakashi had always chosen the latter.

"Kakashi, are you awake?"

Nanara's voice came from the other side of the wooden door, and he sat up.

When he said he could come in, the boy trudged into the room, looking ill at ease.

"I want you to listen to something. I've thought about it... about what to do." He began to speak awkwardly, unsure. "We can't beat the Land of Fire. But...even if we did win the war and take something from the Land of Fire and get rich that way, I think probably no one'd be happy. So, I don't want to fight the Land of Fire...I want us to be friends."

If you truly do aspire to be like the Sixth Hokage...

That's what the prime minister had said. So Nanara decided to try thinking about what the Sixth Hokage would do if he were in Nanara's position. But Kakashi had taught him the answer to that a while ago already. The Sixth Hokage wanted coexistence and coprosperity with the surrounding countries.

"I want to go with the prime minister to the Land of Fire," he said. "Instead of taking anything by force, we should ask for support as equals. ...We'll say we'll pay it back double, for sure."

"I don't suppose it will go well." Kakashi casually rejected this conclusion that Nanara had struggled to reach as he struck a match.

His enthusiasm nipped in the bud, Nanara watched Kakashi light a lamp and scowled. "Why not?"

"If you go with him all by yourself, the prime minister will no doubt end up cajoling you over to his side during the long trip. And you don't have to go all the way to the Land of Fire. There's a much easier way of communicating."

"An easier way of communicating?"

Kakashi pulled out a sheet of parchment and spread it out on the table beneath the lamp. "Paper."

"Huh?" He frowned.

"Friends write each other letters."

"The Land of Fire is far away. How are you planning to deliver a letter?"

Kakashi said nothing and looked toward the window. Ray was sitting on the perch outside, hood over his head.

"Not Ray!" Nanara hurriedly spread his hands out and stepped out as if to protect Ray.

"Why not? A hawk could be in the Land of Fire in two days."

"I can't send him outside the country. He's special. He's the royal hawk!"

"Why is he special because he's the royal hawk?" Kakashi asked. "How is he different from other hawks?"

Nanara gulped, at a loss for words.

Kakashi held out one arm toward Ray. The hawk flapped its wings, legs together, and grabbed onto his arm.

"It wouldn't be the first time he's gone to the Land of Fire. I found this in the previous king's office." Kakashi set a scroll of paper on the table.

Nanara was baffled, wondering when exactly Kakashi had snuck into the off-limits office as he unrolled the scroll. His father's name popped up at the top, written in ink.

"A letter? Weird shape..."

Who was it from? He unrolled the page all the way, saw the name of the sender at the end, and his jaw dropped.

The Sixth Hokage.

That was indeed the signature at the end of the letter in masterful brush strokes.

"It seems that the king corresponded with the Sixth Hokage," Kakashi said.

Nanara's hands on the scroll began to tremble. He couldn't believe it. It was impossible. There was no way. His father had been corresponding with *the* Sixth Hokage?!

"Kakashi!" he cried. "The Sixth Hokage really exists!"

"Mm hmm." Kakashi nodded. "The prime minister said so too."

Nanara's cheeks flushed, and he stroked the spots of ink on the browning paper.

So this was the Sixth Hokage's handwriting.

He shivered, feeling like he was somehow touching a legend. He felt like the slightly loose hand also resembled Kakashi's writing a bit. The letter used lots of difficult characters, and he couldn't read all of them, but there was a spot where "Shuigu" was written in katakana. Apparently, his father had even talked to the Sixth Hokage about the Shuigu.

"Ray. Did you carry letters to the Land of Fire?" Nanara asked, and Ray puffed his chest out proudly, almost like he understood the words.

The next morning, Nanara was groaning in front of a piece of parchment spread out on the table.

How should he start the letter?

"Dear Sixth Hokage"? "Master Sixth Hokage"?

"Unnh..."

Racking his brains, Nanara carefully marked the page with one character after another, the fruit of his studies.

His sister and the prime minister were planning a war against the Land of Fire. He wanted to stop them. He thought there would be civil war. When the fighting ended, he wanted to do whatever he could to avoid a situation where the country was torn apart and the people were starving. He wanted support with rations and resources. Once the country was back on its feet, he would absolutely pay it back.

He had worked so hard on this text, so he wrestled with

whether to sign it with his own name, but in the end, he decided to simply write, "A representative of the Land of Redaku."

Lord Sixth Hokage.

He stared at the name of the recipient at the top and felt something warm and fuzzy.

What would he do if he got an answer? He'd be in trouble if he didn't, but if he got a reply in the Hokage's own hand, he might die of sheer joy. Maybe it was indecent to be happy about all of this, but that was the truth of how he felt. Which made him feel a bit weird.

"I can't believe *this* is what I'm writing about in my first letter to my beloved Sixth Hokage," Nanara muttered.

Kakashi looked surprised. "Did you have other things you wanted to write about?"

"Well, yeah."

The truth was, he didn't want to write a letter of entreaty, he wanted to write a fan letter. About how much he liked the Sixth Hokage, about how entranced he was by his story, about how much courage it gave him. Even if he had ten pieces of parchment, he'd never be able to get it all down.

Nanara rolled up the finished letter, tied it with grass, and hooked it onto Ray's talons.

"Okay, Ray. If you meet the Sixth Hokage, please say a super huge hello for me!"

Ray let out a brief screech as if to say he had it under control and then flew out the window.

Nanara watched the brown feathers fade in the distance, and then he noticed crooked lines here and there along the spine of the mountain.

It couldn't be.

He squinted and gasped when he realized what the lines were.

"Why... It's too soon..."

The army of the prime minister and the queen was closing in on Nagare.

•

The prime minister's army marched through the mountains and was almost upon Nagare on the morning of the second day.

The vanguard was the shinobi squad, clad in sober costumes and on nimble feet. They were supposed to be moving in secret, and the fact that they came happily trekking over the mountain in broad daylight was either a strategy to intimidate Nanara and the villagers, or it meant that they didn't think there would be any resistance here right from the start. Either way, their arrival was several weeks earlier than what Nanara had been told.

But this was not the only thing that was not what it was promised to be.

This was no fifty people.

Trailing after the shinobi were columns of artillerymen. Masses of cylindrical steel were piled up on the carts that the men took turns pushing.

"Cannons," Kakashi murmured.

A weapon particular to a region between the Land of Fire and the Land of Redaku. A device for launching at high speed a lead ball from a steel cylinder, it used a powdered mineral called phosphate for the motive force. Because phosphate did extraordinarily poorly in humid conditions, cannons weren't used in the Five Great Nations. This was the first time Kakashi had ever seen the real thing.

The prime minister had no doubt brought back the manufacturing method for cannons from his tour abroad. At a glance, the total number of artillerymen closing in on Nagare was about three hundred. And roughly forty cannons.

"Are the shinobi carrying the cannons?" Nanara asked Kakashi, as he looked down on the plains from the village watchtower.

"No, judging from their movements, they're not shinobi. I think they're just citizens who have been conscripted."

"You think they're going to attack the Land of Fire with those cannons?"

"No." Kakashi shook his head. "Even carrying the cannons this far is quite a lot of heavy labor. The prime minister must know it's not practical to carry them all the way to the distant Land of Fire."

"So then why would they..."

"Most likely to contain Nagare." The furrow in Kakashi's brow grew deeper as he continued. "It would be a serious problem if you were to stage a coup d'état while the queen and the prime minister are away. The prime minister probably wants to station the cannons in the village together with a commander he has under his thumb."

"That's just..."

There was no way Nagare, a village of not even 150 people, had enough stores to be able to provide rations for such a large army.

Nanara's expression grew stern and he glared at the advancing army. "He's going to ruin us...and keep any rebellion from happening."

By the time noon rolled around, the army had arrived at Nagare.

They settled onto the plains that stretched out to the west and south of the village and began pitching camp.

The prime minister leisurely entered Nagare with several shinobi in tow as bodyguards, and from his horse, announced loudly to the assembled villagers, "This is an order from Her

Majesty the Queen to the village of Nagare. The queen's army will be marching to the east. Thus, you will provide rations—"

"Prime minister, listen to me." Nanara stepped out in front of him. "I'm opposed to this war. I think we can't win, and even if we do, there's no point in it."

The villagers were stunned and looked at Nanara as if to say they hadn't heard anything about disobeying the prime minister.

"You need not worry. Reinforcements will be coming," the prime minister replied coolly.

"Reinforcements?" Nanara asked. "Did you hire more shinobi?"

"They are not shinobi." The prime minister turned his gaze toward the north. The mountain ridges kept going, spreading from the north to the east. Nanara was pretty sure an astronomical research institute had been in that area since ancient times.

"What do you mean?" he asked, but the prime minister ignored him and looked around at the villagers.

"Take whatever food stores you have in the village to the encampment. Make sure you bring out all your winter stores as well," he commanded haughtily and left, as if to say his mission there was complete.

The villagers stared in silence at the departing prime minister.

"There'll be nothing left for us to eat..."

"That's just how it is," Margo encouraged the woman who was on the verge of tears. "We just have to do as he says, and this can end peacefully. If we go up into the mountains, we can still forage wild vegetables out there, and there's also fish to catch."

While she was no doubt trying to think positively, Margo's face was strained. Nanara also knew that there was definitely not enough wild vegetables or fish in this region to keep all of the villagers alive.

Nanara made up his mind. "We're not giving them the stores," he said.

"What?" Margo said, stunned.

"If this was a necessary fight, I'd support it," he continued. "But the prime minister just wants to invade. We can't help him do that."

"So then, what should we do?"

"We stop them. With force."

The villagers couldn't grasp what Nanara was saying.

"We're going to fight?" Kakashi asked.

Nanara nodded.

It would have been a lie to say that he wasn't afraid. But he had written in his letter to the Sixth Hokage that he wanted support because he was going to fight. He couldn't exactly renege on those words.

"Yes. We fight."

"In that case, I'll help you to the extent that I can." Kakashi clasped his hands together in front of his chest. He locked his fingers into strange shapes two or three times, almost like he was making shadow animals. And then he slammed a hand against the ground.

The earth shook slightly, and Nanara looked around. "Hm?"

The next few seconds were a blur.

The ground around the village slid toward the sky, kicking up dust, and became a wall the height of a small hill in the blink of an eye. The northeast of Nagare had always been backed by a steep cliff, but now the west and south were encircled by a dirt wall, so that the village was protected 360 degrees by wall and cliff. While the wall was rumbling upward, Nanara saw a shinobi with quick reflexes throw something like a kunai, but it was easily bounced back by the dirt wall.

"What is... Huh? Kakashi? You did this?" Nanara looked at the wall, looked at Kakashi, looked at the wall, and looked at Kakashi once more.

A powerful defensive dirt wall. It was almost like that thing he'd read about in the book, the Sixth Hokage's Earth Style. Mud Wall.

"Kakashi... You... You can't be..." Nanara's voice shook.

Kakashi braced himself and turned to face Nanara.

"You can't really be—a ninja like the Sixth Hokage?!"

"...Yes."

There was a curious pause. But Kakashi had assented, at any rate, so Nanara accepted that his tutor was a shinobi and his eyes shone.

"Wow... You're a ninja." His eyes were suddenly sparkling about a hundred percent more than normal.

"I'll tell you right now that I'm not going to apologize for hiding who I am," Kakashi said in a totally regular sort of tone, as he looked around at the stunned villagers.

On the plains, the prime minister had flown into a rage and was hurling angry shouts at the dirt wall.

"Prince Nanara, what is the meaning of this?! If you do not take this wall down immediately, this will be seen as insurrection!"

"It is an insurrection!" Nanara shouted back from the watchtower. "Nagare does not agree with the war! We will not provide rations!"

While Manari's face lost all its color as she poked her head out of a tent and learned of her brother's rebellion, the prime minister chuckled to himself, as though he had found a just cause for attack and sent a signal to the artillerymen.

They moved as one to turn the carts and point the barrels of the cannons at the mud wall.

"They're really going to attack." Nanara frowned. "Kakashi, we're okay, right?"

"Mm, probably."

Probably? He watched on tenterhooks as the soldiers loaded the cannons. A spark travelled down the fuse and disappeared inside the barrel.

Boom!

Fire and thunder jetted from the barrel, and the cannonball shook the earth as it shot forward, hitting the mud wall squarely and exploding violently. The villagers screamed and crouched down, shielding each other from the inevitable damage.

But the mud wall didn't give an inch. A puff of dust rose up into the air, and the wall around them remained.

"Not even a scratch." The prime minister looked up bitterly at the mud wall.

"This wall is an Earth Style technique." One of the younger shinobi stepped forward. "Shinobi techniques all have their affinities. That's the best point of attack. The weak point of Earth Style is Lightning Style." The man's right hand crackled with electricity.

"What's that technique?" the prime minister asked.

"Lightning Blade. A major jutsu of the Land of Fire, a secret tradition. People still talk of the Sixth Hokage cutting lightning with it." The shinobi smiled confidently and stepped out toward the mud wall.

In general, Earth Style was seen as weak to Lightning Style because the many impurities that existed in the earth were good conductors for electricity.

"Please watch as I smash it with my Lightning Blade."

Watching the shinobi's movements from the watchtower, Nanara panicked. "Kakashi! That guy's trouble! He looks like he's going to use a seriously amazing technique!"

His tutor said nothing.

"Are you listening to me, Kakashi? It's bad! We're in trouble!"

Aah, be quiet.

Kakashi stared intently at the end point of the trajectory that the man's technique would likely follow. He followed his enemy's eyes to its target and concentrated his mind on the point where the attack would likely hit.

The man released the jutsu.

Crack! Crack!

Thunder roared, and the lightning attack hit the wall at the speed of light. The shinobi no doubt thought the wall of earth would crumble to dust when directly hit with Lightning Style.

However.

"What the...?" The shinobi that had launched the lightning attack stared at the mud wall, incredulous.

The instant the electrical charge reached the wall, it was sucked into the earth and disappeared. The place where his attack should have connected was transparent like crystal. And it was only that spot, almost as though the material had been instantly switched from dirt to glass.

While the shinobi blinked in surprise, the see-through area vanished and became dirt once more.

"What was that? It looked like the wall turned transparent, deflected the electrical attack, and...went right back to being dirt."

"It must be some kind of genjutsu," the shinobi snorted. "No need to worry. It takes an enormous amount of chakra to maintain an earth wall this massive. It won't last long. If it's just the one ninja, he'll wear himself down in half a day, and the jutsu will be released."

The man had once been a Land of Fire ninja. He had served during the era of the Sixth Hokage, when people were enthusiastically fusing rapidly developed scientific techniques with the shinobi jutsu passed down and honed through the generations.

In that world, a certain scientist had espoused a counter to Lightning Style for Earth Style.

No, that wasn't just a jutsu. It was a completely unworkable idea, utterly impossible to achieve in reality.

A jutsu to transform a part of the mud wall into glass.

Earth included many of the raw materials for glass. If a ninja were to gather all those glass elements in one spot and rearrange the atomic structure, the mud wall could hypothetically turn to glass in that one area. And because glass was an insulator that did not allow electricity to pass through it, the part that was glass would, in theory, nullify a Lightning Style attack.

The jutsu had been given the name Earth Style, Earth Stone Hero Technique. And the change in the mud wall he'd seen earlier looked to be that very technique.

"But... No, impossible," the man muttered to himself, shaking his head.

The Earth Stone Hero technique was a ninjutsu fantasy, dreamed up by a brainiac scientist who had no idea about the practice of ninjutsu.

It would take an average person years just to train to increase the purity of the glass elements in one spot in the earth. And then to execute it, they'd have to pinpoint the place where the Lightning Style would strike and make the change happen while maintaining the entire mud wall.

On top of that, they would need to return it to its original earth state after repelling the electrical attack with the Earth Stone Hero technique. A glass wall might be able to defend against Lightning Style attacks, but it would easily shatter with a simple physical attack.

Earth Stone Hero was completely unworkable. The speed, the accuracy. It required such quick and accurate chakra control that it made him dizzy just imagining it. A ninja capable of this kind of trick didn't exist...

The man suddenly stopped.

Now that he was thinking about it, the former Hokage of the Land of Fire had been widely praised as a master of all five Styles. If it were him, then maybe...

"No, there's no way." He shook his head to reject this fanciful thought.

The former Hokage was the leading figure in the rapid development of the Land of Fire and in building peace globally. He was a very important person. There was no way he'd stick his nose into a coup d'état out here in the boonies.

"That was not Lightning Blade." Kakashi was thoroughly unbothered as he looked down at the prime minister and the shinobi walking back to the camp.

He didn't particularly care that this shinobi had gone and claimed the name of the technique that had once been his own personal specialty, but the fact was, it had been a fairly simple bit of Lightning Style. Given that the man had managed to stay alive this long as a rogue shinobi, he must have had some decent skills, but they didn't begin to compare to Kakashi's.

Earth Style, Earth Stone Hero. Kakashi had mastered this jutsu to counter Lightning Style when a certain scientist proposed it to him some time ago. He hadn't used it in battle in quite a while, but he thought it had still gone pretty well. The technique changed mud into glass and nullified Lightning Style attacks, but it couldn't repel very strong hits because the heat would melt the glass. If it had been his student Chidori attacking, he wouldn't have been able to defend against the blow completely.

But he had more important things to think about.

He looked back at the villagers, who were milling about in confusion.

"Nanara, you disobeyed the prime minister. And what is this wall?"

"It's still not too late. We can apologize and give them the food. We'll be in serious trouble if we disobey the queen, you know."

The color had drained from all of their faces. And that was no wonder. Their small village had suddenly become a stronghold, and they didn't know if the wall of earth was there to protect or imprison them.

"Aah," Kakashi said. "Okay, please calm down."

The villagers fell silent and peered fearfully at him as though they were seeing a demon.

"I understand your confusion," he continued. "But would you hear Nanara out at least? I know because I went with him to the capital, but it seems like your country's stuck between a rock and a hard place."

"Wait. Aren't you a tutor?" One man looked at Kakashi uneasily. "How come a teacher's using amazing technique like this?"

"Yeah," another man agreed. "You might be popular with the women, but I've heard stories about you. You seem pretty shifty. I mean, you came to Nagare because the prime minister sent you, right? Are you a spy?"

"That's—" Nanara started to respond forcefully, but unable to find the right words, he froze with his mouth open. When he thought about it, the man was right.

"Master Kakashi, who *are* you?" Margo asked nervously. "This wall... It's ninjutsu, isn't it?"

Kakashi shook his head gently. "I'll explain everything

once this fight is over. To put it another way, I *won't* tell you anything until we're done fighting."

"So why can't you tell us?" she asked.

"Because if you're tortured and you let my identity slip, it might expose my country to danger."

Cowed by this disturbing logic, the villagers fell silent.

"Well, anyway. Please listen to what Nanara has to say. Come to your conclusions once you have all the information," Kakashi said and turned on his heel.

"Where are you going?" Nanara asked anxiously.

"It'll be easier for the villagers to talk with each other without an outsider like me around."

That Kakashi really was a fishy guy.

Nanara felt this keenly after talking with the villagers. He walked around the village, looking for the fishy man in question.

To start with, he didn't know the first thing about him. When he asked about anything personal, Kakashi simply dodged the question. Now that he thought about it, he doubted Kakashi had even been sent from the capital.

But for some reason, he wanted to trust him. He wanted to follow him. He was sure that when people talked about a great leader, they meant someone like Kakashi.

"I talked to everyone. I told them about the capital, all that stuff," he reported when he found Kakashi sitting on a bale of hay, reading a book.

"How'd it go?" his tutor asked.

"They said they need time to digest it all. We decided to meet again tomorrow morning and talk then."

"I can understand why they'd be hesitant," Kakashi said,

closing his book. "After the prime minister made such a show of how much battle power they have, it's only natural to be afraid of turning on the queen. It would be great if we had some kind of support."

"Support?" Nanara murmured, looking up at the evening sky, where the sun seemed reluctant to set on them.

Ray still hadn't come back.

•

The next morning, forty cannons had been set up around them in a semicircle. All the barrels were pointed squarely at the village, practically commanding them to surrender.

Nanara looked down on the encampment at the foot of the village with dark feelings. He could see the crimson gown of the prime minister moving through the camp, but he could find no sign of his sister. She was probably locked away in a tent somewhere.

The threat of the cannons stirred up a serious fear in the villagers. Nanara talked with them once more in the plaza about their course of action, but even after sleeping on it, the group urging surrender remained the overwhelming majority. Margo in particular refused to fight the prime minister. She wanted to be able to return to the capital again one day.

That said, it was obvious to all that if they fed an army of people, they'd hit the bottom of their stores in no time flat.

They were boxed in on all sides.

"What should we do?" Margo said, on the verge of tears.

A middle-aged man crossed his arms and sighed. "What-ever else, the fact is that prime minister there got ahold of this much power somehow. Isn't that the real issue here? It was the old king who appointed him."

Nanara froze.

"There's no point in bringing that up now," Margo chided him, but the man didn't stop.

"If we take it all the way back, the problem is that the old king was incompetent, hm? I mean trusting a man like that, giving him this appointment, utterly idiotic—"

"Don't you say that about my father!" Nanara shouted, unable to stop himself even though he knew this was no time to be making enemies.

He felt everyone's eyes settle on him, but he was feeling so many powerful things that he couldn't control himself.

For a second, the man was shocked into silence, but then he grinned and shrugged. "Come on, Nanara. Don't get in a stink about it. You can't be mad. It's the truth."

"You shut your mouth!" He leaned forward, ready to grab hold of the man.

"Calm down," came Kakashi's voice from above his head. He squirmed as he realized that Kakashi had caught him from behind. "Let go, Kakashi! This man doesn't know the first thing about my father!"

He was dragged away helplessly out of the plaza. Kakashi tucked Nanara under his arm while the boy shouted to be let go, climbed a hill, and finally set him down with a *thump* after they had reached the watchtower at the far edge of the village.

"My father was not incompetent!" Nanara protested force-fully, as soon as his feet were on the ground again. "He worked hard for this country his whole life!"

Kakashi sighed. "Anyone would get mad at someone saying bad things about their family. I get that. But whatever happens, you're a member of the royal family, and you can't go laying hands on a citizen."

"The royal family's fake," Nanara spat. "We're no different

from anyone else. And it's weird that we get to stand above people just because we're the 'royal family.'"

"Maybe so," Kakashi said. "But according to that villager back there, your father was a bit subpar as king."

"He was not!" Nanara shouted, his eyes red. He couldn't believe even Kakashi was saying this. "You never even met him. Don't just go saying stuff! My father wasn't subpar. Everyone respected him. They needed him! No matter how busy he was, he never, ever slacked off. He was always thinking about all of them first—"

"He was a wonderful king?"

"He was." His voice wobbled.

Kakashi looked down at him. "If the previous king was so wonderful, then why didn't you inherit the throne? Didn't you want to be like your father?"

"It's not that!"

Kakashi seemed to be pushing him. He wouldn't wait for Nanara to find the words himself like he usually did.

"It's the opposite... I *do* want to be like him. But I wasn't sure I could be... So I—"

"So you didn't become king?"

Nanara took a step back. He wanted to stop talking about this, and yet he couldn't let it go. Kakashi was dredging up all the feelings he'd been pretending not to notice, the not-quite-quenched embers of a fire charring a wood pile, burning slowly but surely.

"You're not king now, but you're trying to persuade everyone to go against the prime minister," Kakashi noted. "Why is that?"

"It's..."

"Why do you want to protect this country? You're not the king or anything."

"But I'm my father's son!" Tears finally spilled out of Nanara's eyes.

Even if he couldn't believe in the reality of the royal family, Nanara had grown up proudly watching the king. As his father's son, he wanted to protect the country his father loved.

"If my sister—the queen is about to step off the path, then I want to stop her! I'm sure Dad would think the same thing."

What popped into his mind was the face of the girl who had been hit because of him. Ever since he'd seen the people suffering in the capital, his desire to protect this country, the land built up by his ancestors and his father, had only grown stronger.

Nanara exhaled, half-groaning. "I really want to protect this country. But...I don't know if I'm good enough. I mean...like, the Hokage isn't chosen by blood, but by actual power."

"I absolutely get what you're saying." Kakashi crouched down and met Nanara's eyes. "Blood can be really annoying. You can't choose it, and you can't change it. But if you can't choose what family you're born into, you need to at least face that family and the blood you inherited if you can. You have this blood. Your only option is to do everything in your power with it."

What to do with the things you inherit from your parents—this was a deeply meaningful question when it came to living as a ninja as well.

There were special abilities passed down through families in the ninja world, and they were incredibly powerful. The Uchiha blood. The Hyuga Byakugan. And although the biju tailed beast chakra wasn't inherited, it fell into a similar category, in the sense that it was a power gained without seeking it.

The faces of his students and colleagues popped up in the back of his mind. All of them lived earnestly in the face of these

inheritances, sometimes proud, other times fiercely loathing the very thought of them. Just like how a thick-browed training fool faced the fact that he was not blessed with the talent for ninjutsu by building strength through his own efforts.

Nanara fell silent and dropped his gaze to the ground.

As he watched over him, Kakashi unconsciously touched his left eye. An unusual ability had once been housed in that eye, a "present" given to him by a dear friend. Once mastered, this eye had unparalleled power, but unfortunately it was an inherited kekkei genkai, and Kakashi's own physical nature made it difficult for him to wield the eye very effectively.

Nonetheless, Kakashi had never stopped confronting this ability that ill-suited his body.

Your body is not of the tribe this eye belongs to.

An Uchiha man said this to him once, a long time ago. And Kakashi knew that full well. But he continued to hone this ability that he couldn't use properly and eventually became so proficient with it that people began to call him "Kakashi of the Sharingan." He put in this work because he wanted to see the world with the eye that his dear friend gave him in his final moments—or at least what he thought were his final moments. It was none other than Obito himself who had given Kakashi a will powerful enough to overcome the barrier of blood.

"What do you think it is that makes a leader a leader, a king a king?" Nanara asked slowly, the words dropping from his mouth. "I was born with the blood of the royal family... But how can I... become like the Sixth Hokage, when he was chosen to become leader?"

"All you can do is gain recognition through your actions. You have to forge bonds with the people around you," Kakashi said and turned his gaze out the window.

"Look." He pointed to the distant sky. "Ray's coming back."

Nanara lifted his face with a gasp.

The hawk was there, dark brown wings spread, flying boldly through the air.

"Ray!" Nanara shouted, waving both arms.

When he looked up at Ray, the hawk looked the same as any other hawk. And yet Ray was the royal hawk. Not because his parents had been royal hawks, but because he had a bond with the previous king and now with Nanara.

The letter Ray brought from the Land of Fire said that they were preparing support in response to Nanara's request. They would help however they could with provisions, medical supplies, and anything else they had to offer.

Nanara slowly read one character after the other in the Hokage's letter, very nearly in tears. When he at last came to the name written at the end, his jaw dropped.

The Seventh Hokage.

That was what it said in the very distinctive handwriting.

"There's a new one!" he cried.

"There was a change in leadership," Kakashi said.

Nanara's hand shook. "Did he die?"

Kakashi shrugged. "He might have gotten old and retired."

"Oh," Nanara sighed with relief. "I'm sure that's it. The Sixth Hokage worked so hard, he should get some time to just relax."

He stroked the Hokage's signature on the letter. His real name was also written there, below his title. "The Seventh Hokage, Uzumaki Naruto." It was a weird name, but he felt a strange light in it.

For a while, Nanara simply stared at the Hokage's handwriting, his face beet red. Eventually, however, he was unable to completely contain his excitement, and he ran out into the plaza, clutching the letter.

"Everyone! Look at this! A letter from the Hokage!"

The name of the legendary Hokage had more than enough power to give the villagers a push in the right direction. The Seventh Hokage of the Land of Fire had promised support. This gave many villagers the courage to stand up to the prime minister. Not all of them, of course. But in the end, a majority of the villagers agreed to fight.

The decisive battle would be that night.

•

Kakashi watched as Nanara ran out toward the plaza with the letter in hand and leaned back against the watchtower. He took his mask off and loosened his collar as he slid down to the ground and let out a long sigh.

He had been using this Earth Style technique for over a day and a half now.

His power had grown by leaps and bounds compared with the days when he had fought Obito and Madara. This was only natural given that many years had passed, and he had devoted himself to his training during that time. He had lost the Sharingan and could no longer use Lightning Blade, but he had gained many new techniques in their place, and his chakra had also grown orders of magnitude from what it had been back then. Even so, maintaining a Mud Wall large enough to encircle an entire village and strong enough to resist cannon attacks was totally and utterly exhausting.

He wiped away the sweat on his brow, his breathing shallow.

Kakashi had about four Lightning Blades' worth of chakra left to keep the wall up until the battle that night.

Chapter 4

In the middle of the night, Nanara, Kakashi, and the villagers gathered in front of the mud wall. It would be dawn in a few hours. Fortunately, the moon was hidden behind thick clouds— the poor visibility worked in their favor. They had the advantage of knowing the terrain.

"Everyone's been evacuated," communications officer Margo came to Nanara to report.

"Thanks. You should evacuate now too," he told her.

Margo was not in favor of disobeying the prime minister, and as such she was supposed to evacuate to the rear with all the other villagers who were opposed. But in the end, she shook off her opposition and put the pot in her hands on her head as armor.

"I'm going to fight. If I let you fight all by yourself and lived to return to the capital, I could never show my face again."

Nanara swallowed the urge to ask if she was sure and nodded.

Margo wasn't alone; the other villagers there were all wearing pots or baskets on their heads and were armed with makeshift weapons. They clutched hoes and scythes, and full leather water bags hung from their waists.

The strategy was simple. Kakashi would take on the shinobi. During that time, the villagers would infiltrate the encampment and wet the ammunition powder needed to fire the cannons, rendering it useless. Meanwhile, Nanara would go off on his own to look for the queen and persuade her to abandon the advance.

"You're all ready then?" Kakashi asked, and the party nodded.

He locked his hands together in front of his chest.

Thwwm. The earth shook silently. The wall in front of them began to break down, crumbling to pieces. The Mud Wall technique had been released.

"Let's go!" Nanara leaped forward. Sumure was quick to follow, and the other villagers ran behind them.

•

The camp was quiet. The majority of the shinobi not on guard duty were asleep in their tents.

Hoo! an owl called.

One man had left his tent to answer the call of nature when he felt the earth shudder. For a moment, he wondered if the Mud Wall technique had been undone, but the vibration was far too small for that. The release of the chakra to create a wall that huge would come with some serious shaking and a loud roar. Even if the ninja who wielded it was a true master.

He'd probably just had too much to drink and stumbled a bit. Assured, the man leisurely finished his business and headed back to his tent. And stopped in his tracks.

The Earth Style wall around the village had been released. "Wha..."

To be more precise, it had melted away. The mud wall had

been large enough to surround an entire village, and yet each and every one of those grains of sand had quietly vanished, simply disappearing in the air. Without even a puff of dust. This was incredible chakra control.

Lost in admiration, the rogue ninja was caught unaware when someone hit him abruptly from behind. His knees gave out and he crumpled to the ground.

"Kaw..." It was a hoarse attempt at signaling alarm. His body was numb to the core. He couldn't move a single finger.

The last thing he saw from behind his descending eyelids was a ninja with hair that was silver like a wolf's shining in the moonlight and a gaze sleepy like a goat's.

The rogue shinobi that the prime minister had assembled lacked a cohesive ethos that would inspire them to fight or protect. They were simply mercenaries. They would, of course, dutifully carry out their mission, even if it meant sacrificing their lives, but such sacrifice was not preferred. On the other hand, the peasants who carried the cannons on the long road to protect the capital had greater morale.

The shinobi standing watch on the east side of the encampment was charged to monitor the village and look for any subtle movement. However, they were much more engrossed in a game of shogi than in keeping an eye out for enemy action.

"Who's winning?"

"Hmm, not sure here," the man replied absentmindedly, completely caught up in the game. As he stared at the board, he suddenly wondered who had just spoken, and he lifted his head.

He saw his opponent across from him frothing at the mouth. The man who had been watching the contest from behind him was on the ground.

"Huh?" He felt a slight impact on the back of his neck, and the game piece dropped from his hand as he flopped forward on the board.

Meanwhile, the three shinobi keeping watch on the north side were somewhat more serious about their duties than the men on the east side. They turned their attention to the wall around the village from time to time, but they were mainly watching the cliff to the north, with the idea that the villagers might take a detour and come around that way.

"I can't believe this village has an ally like that, a shinobi so amazing they can keep a Mud Wall that big going for this long."

"Nah, there's no way it's just one person. It's gotta be a combo technique with a bunch of shinobi."

"I guess maybe."

As they chatted, one of the men casually looked over his shoulder.

The mud wall was blanketed in darkness, and he couldn't see it. But he sensed people moving between the village and the encampment.

He stood up with a gasp, raised his torch, and narrowed his eyes. And realized that the mud wall had come down.

"Oy! The villagers—" *Are moving*, the man started to say when someone grabbed him firmly from behind. A fist hit him squarely in the chest, knocking the air out of his lungs and dragging his consciousness along with it.

"Hm?"

"You say something?"

Just as his remaining comrades also noticed something was off, hands abruptly clamped onto their heads and slammed them together. A dull *kunk*. Knocked unconscious in a mutual head butt, the two ninja rolled their eyes back and passed out.

Kakashi stamped out the light of the lookout's torch.

The prime minister had hired fifty shinobi in total.

"Forty-three to go then," he muttered and dropped the two now lump-headed shinobi to the ground. Then he pulled the headband with the mark of Konoha down diagonally to cover his left eye before turning and sneaking toward the silent tents.

The prime minister's shinobi were not a gang of weaklings. They had made it this far as rogue shinobi without dying, so they couldn't have been novice jutsu users.

Kakashi held his breath and slipped inside a tent. There were ten shinobi inside, all dozing, sitting with one knee up or cross-legged.

This was a group that had trained to wake at the sound of a cat's step. He made himself invisible and slid among them, still holding his breath, and carefully landed a hand strike on each enemy's neck from one end to the other. The sleep-inducing chakra point Iruka had taught him was helpful. The technique rendered enemies helpless without killing them.

Before he became Hokage, Kakashi had only known how to kill people. He had methods of capturing people without killing them, but they all involved pain and torture. But as time wore on and the country grew stable, the shinobi principle of capture without killing had taken favor. And it was none other than the Sixth Hokage himself who had struggled with how to write the guidelines for this new no-kill capture policy. He'd discussed it with Iruka, the principal of the academy at the time, and he had laughed. Kakashi remembered every single word of what he said.

"It's okay. It might not look it, but we do more than just teach students at the academy. We've saved jutsu to make an enemy fall asleep instantly or freeze them on the spot. Everything from old to new is right here."

Distracted by the memory of Iruka's proud face, Kakashi

accidentally allowed a bit of fabric to rustle while strangling the ninth shinobi.

A man sleeping further back in the tent with one knee up snapped his eyes open at the sound, and as soon as he saw Kakashi, started thrusting a hand into his jacket to pull out a dagger. He whirled around, slashed the tent open, and shouted, "Intruder! Wake up!"

Kakashi's hand came down over the man's mouth. He used his other hand to strangle him to unconsciousness. After a few seconds, the body grew limp and fell to the ground, and Kakashi stepped outside through the opening the man had cut in the tent.

Men in shinobi garb were lined up before him. Five, he guessed before they were joined by another two to become seven.

Aah, everyone's awake now...

The camp was no longer quiet. The cacophony came from the non-shinobi soldiers.

"It's an enemy attack. Put out the torches!"

"No, don't do that!"

They ran around in confusion, causing chaos. Meanwhile, the seven shinobi who had arrived first on the scene said nothing as they carefully closed the distance between themselves and Kakashi.

He wanted a weapon. He groped around and touched a pot hanging under one of the watchfire baskets.

"Mm." He frowned. "Well! I guess this'll do."

It had been a while since he'd fought against shinobi, but he didn't have the time to have a nice leisurely go of it. He was one against fifty. If he didn't settle this before it turned into a group brawl, he might not make it out unscathed.

"Let's get to it then," Kakashi said to himself and kicked at the ground.

Just one?

The shinobi man had raced over when he heard the news but snorted in disdain when he saw the intruder. Wandering in on his own without a plan, surrounded by a group of ninja in the blink of an eye—this guy was no great threat. He was tall if nothing else, but he looked sort of sleepy.

Even as he mentally let his guard down, the man unsheathed his sword cautiously. He held it low in front of him and dropped into a crouch. He imagined thrusting it into the stomach of the man before him, slicing him in two, and licked his lips.

Clang!

One of his comrades was suddenly on his back.

"Uh?"

He suddenly felt a powerfully bloodthirsty presence before him. He quickly looked back and found the intruder standing there. A fist slammed into his side, and his hand let go of the hilt of his sword.

He's going to kill me!

He braced himself for death as he crumpled to the ground, but the intruder pulled away for some reason. He pitched forward to pick up his sword and readied it in front of him once more, back against the wall.

Clang!

He heard the metallic sound again from somewhere, and another of his allies dropped, hands still clasped together about to weave a sign.

A flat piece of metal flashed briefly in the darkness.

What was that? A disc weapon?

Clang!

The sound rang out again, and a shinobi clutching a kunai staggered and fell.

This time, he saw it clearly. The ninja had been hit by a pot lid, the iron kind used for cooking rice. When the rice got stuck to it, it was almost impossible to get off. He hated that.

...A pot lid?

Clang. Clang.

Two faces, eyes rolling back in their heads, slammed into the ground. The pot lid left a silver afterimage before melting once more into the darkness.

The man readied his blade, unable to process the fact that his comrades were being taken down one after the other by a pot lid. It must have been some amazing pot lid that used chakra. That had to be it.

The tip of his blade wiggling, he inched backward. His back touched the wooden post of the tripod that held the watchfire pot.

"Where's he coming from?" he murmured to himself.

And then he heard a sixth *clang* and the sound of his ally hitting the dirt. At last, a cold sweat sprang up on his forehead. He was the only one still standing. In mere seconds, a fight that started as seven against one had turned into a one-on-one battle.

In the darkness, his whole body on high alert, blood vessels threatening to boil over, he peered out into the area. All his comrades had been felled with a single blow. If he got hit now, it was all over.

Hyoo! He felt iron cut through the air above his head.

"Gaaah!" The man thrust the sword he was holding in reverse upward, half-crazed.

He felt it hit. He saw the pot lid fly off, repelled by the tip of his blade.

He felt a surge of excitement. He'd won. His guard loosened, even though he hadn't confirmed his win yet.

He felt a weight on his chest and looked down to find a

kunai thrust deep into his heart. He was about to cry out in shock and pain when the kunai vanished.

"Huh?" He realized it was genjutsu, but he was still baffled for a moment.

That was all it took. A half second later, he took a palm strike to his neck and lost consciousness.

"So that's twenty-six more to go."

Kakashi picked up the weapon that had been knocked away and let out a sigh. The rounded pot lid had performed surprisingly well, but it had indeed been unable to withstand that last sword strike. It was now squashed flat. *Might be good against bullets,* he assessed optimistically and tucked it away in his pocket for now.

Now that he'd gone up against a few of these shinobi, it seemed their average ability was on the special jonin level. They weren't weak, and a couple had more advanced abilities he'd expect in a rogue shinobi, but to Kakashi, they were a group of small-time punks.

"Well, that last one with the sword handled himself pretty well, I guess."

Because the man had shown surprising tenacity, Kakashi had been forced to use genjutsu and exhaust his little remaining chakra, although he'd hoped to keep aside at least a bit for when he faced the prime minister.

He could sense more shinobi charging in, so Kakashi quenched his aura and slid into the darkness once more.

The six shinobi were all in a group, compensating for each other's blind spots and watching the area carefully. It hadn't

even been a minute since they heard the voice shouting about an intruder. And in that same time, seven of their comrades had lost consciousness.

"Probably the Land of Fire or a shinobi from a country around there," the man running in the lead muttered.

"Yes," said a younger man who was not far behind him.

None of their fallen comrades had been dealt a killing blow. It would have been faster and easier for this intruder to just kill, and yet he didn't. Such eccentric behavior could only have been a shinobi from one of the Five Great Nations centered around the Land of Fire.

"Seven guys taken out at one time means there's probably more than one intruder. At least three—no, four, maybe."

"Yeah. There was barely any sign of resistance either, so they likely took one man each and thrashed them. Our enemy's sharp, to be sure, but that doesn't change the fact that there are more of us."

When the group passed by, the watchfire in the iron pot swung wildly and fell. One of the shinobi should have caught it and hung it back up, but the young man closest to it pulled back, afraid of burning his hands.

The burning wood scattered all over the ground. The fire continued to burn on the sand, but their surroundings grew noticeably darker. Suddenly unable to see, the shinobi were late to react to the shadow that cut in front of them.

Whud.

Something hard hit the skull of the man in the lead, and his eyes rolled back as he fell down.

The limp bodies of his comrades landed on his chest one after the other. One, two, three, four people. The young man became the last one standing when he heard the fifth man next to him get cracked on the head.

"Aah, another one wrecked," the intruder said with a sigh and tossed something aside.

The young man wasn't so foolish as to follow it with his gaze and create an opening for the intruder to attack, but he did catch it out of the corner of his eye. Maybe it was just his imagination, but it looked like a crushed pot. He didn't have the luxury of double-checking.

Gripping a kunai, the man faced off against the intruder.

"You scoundrel, disobeying the queen... I'm not letting you leave alive!" He was trying to be threatening, but his voice shook. Face to face with the intruder on his own, he felt the waves of intimidation and understood for the first time that his opponent was a monster on an entirely different level.

The intruder had his face covered with a headband and a mask over his mouth, so the young man couldn't really see what he looked like. But he felt like he had seen him somewhere before.

If this masked intruder was a shinobi famous enough to cover his face, he as a rogue shinobi would be outmatched. He would have already fled, but he had a duty to hold the intruder's attention for as long as possible, until backup arrived.

"I'm not letting you leave alive," he spat again and dropped his hips. He had given up on using jutsu. The intruder was too well guarded, and he was pretty sure he wouldn't even get the chance to finish weaving a sign.

The intruder was silent. Apparently, he had no intention of making pointless talk and buying some time.

The young man readied his kunai in front of him and stared at the intruder unblinking.

Clank.

Something twisted around his ankle, and in the next breath, his body was dancing up into the air.

Yanked up off the ground by a weighted chain, the young man caught sight of a new comrade charging in out of the corner of his eye.

He threw a shuriken, and the intruder grabbed the shoulders of the man hanging in space, pushing him forward.

Is he using me as a shield against the shuriken?!

But the intruder only caught the incoming shuriken with the long fingers extending from his glove and tossed it back.

Huh? he thought when he was hit in the back of the neck. Still not understanding what was going on, he slipped out of consciousness like he was falling into a deep sleep.

The shuriken the intruder threw back went through the man's foot. He lost his balance and reeled helplessly backward. In the blink of an eye, the intruder closed the distance between them and ripped into him with a knee strike.

The intruder dodged another shinobi coming at him with a punch as he stuck out a foot and tripped him, without a hint of malice, before melting into the darkness once more.

"No spreading out. Stick together!"

"No blind spots!"

Roars echoed in the night, and the shinobi put their backs together, on guard in all directions.

"Where's he going to come from..." came a murmur from somewhere.

The moonlight flickered ever so slightly in the shadow cast by the wall.

There!

One man grabbed the neck of a smaller comrade beside him and threw him as hard as he could toward the base of the fence. The shadow shuddered, and the intruder flew out, sidestepping the small man and leaping off to one side.

The small ninja abruptly used as a projectile nevertheless quickly adapted to the situation, kicking at the wall to change his position and fly at the intruder.

He pulled a cloth from his jacket as a blind and immediately wove a sign. The small man's specialty was Wind Style.

He would launch a low pressure cyclone and use the difference in air pressure to crush his enemy's windpipe.

A Wind Style air current began to rotate turbulently between the hands he held in front of his chest.

Unfortunately for him, however, the intruder was faster than the wind. His knee dug into the small man's groin, causing him to groan helplessly. The back of his neck was wide open. A palm strike came down on it, and he groaned no more.

The shinobi to the rear had finished weaving his signs. The spear he held was suddenly wrapped in blue flames from handle to tip.

"Fire Style! Fire Spear! Get ready!" he barked and charged the intruder.

Two of his comrades readied their swords to either side of him and provided backup. If the three of them flew at the intruder at the same time, at least one of them would graze him with a blade.

He'd expected the intruder to use the small unconscious man as a shield and come at them, but he didn't do that. The small man still flat on the ground, the intruder tossed a small white ball down at his feet.

There was an explosion, and the area was blanketed in smoke.
Bad move, guy.

The spear man grinned. Maybe the intruder had used the smoke bomb out of desperation, but it only gave him and his comrades the advantage. In a situation like this, it was the intruder who would end up having nowhere to run.

The flame-covered spear slashed horizontally. Through the opening in the smoke, he saw one of his comrades collapse. The intruder moved slowly behind him. From the movement of his

eyes, he could tell that he was gauging the temperature and air pressure of the burning spear.

In a flash, the man on the left attacked with his sword. The intruder quickly pulled a kunai from the pocket of the fallen man and caught the blow, but the man on the left pushed back and sliced at his jacket. But the intruder fled upward, moving like an animal, and of all things, came to stand on the wrist of the man holding the sword.

"Huh..." The man's face drooped, like all the fight had gone out of him. He felt the weight on his wrist followed by a kick slammed into his face, and then he passed out.

Now it was one-on-one. Only the man with the spear was still standing.

Smoke blocking his field of view, the intruder whirled around and sent his gaze to the rear.

The spear stood upright in the earth, still burning.

"...!"

For the first time, the eyes of the expressionless intruder widened.

Gotcha!

The shinobi sliced at the intruder from his blind spot with a short spear. The intruder reacted to the wind pressure and whirled around, but he was just barely too late.

While he'd been dispatching the men with swords charging from either side, the intruder had been keeping an eye on the position of the flaming lance. The shinobi had dared to toss it away to use as a decoy, so that he could get the back of this fearsomely sharp intruder for even just a second.

The naked blade caught the intruder's throat, and fresh blood welled up.

I win!

A moment after he declared his victory, something drove deep into his solar plexus. He fell forward into the drops of

blood and realized he'd taken a knee strike. He was certain that he'd cut the man's throat, and yet it was the thigh of his fallen comrade spurting blood.

Genjutsu?

He dropped a knee to the ground and gasped when he saw the face of the intruder through the smoke for the first time.

Shockingly silver hair and sharp eyes reminiscent of a bird of prey. Strong features stood out clearly through the cloth covering his face. And the headband worn diagonally to hide the left eye. The spear-user shinobi had seen this face any number of times in broadcasts of the Five Shadows Summit, in articles about the retirement of the Sixth Hokage...

"You...can't be..."

The intruder was the Sixth Hokage. He had to tell his comrades right away, but the problem was that the man could no longer so much as twitch. The sweet scent of the smoke bomb had seeped deep into his bones, and his thoughts quickly receded.

At the same time as the man let go of consciousness, the flaming spear in the ground went out with a whine.

Fourteen left.

Blood in his silver hair, the intruder emerged from the white smoke shimmering like a mirage. He lowered a bloodstained blade, and one side of his face was covered in a blood splatter. A man watched, the nail to be hammered into this chilling figure, the living personification of an evil spirit.

There was no mistake. It was the Sixth Hokage. Hatake Kakashi... The man never dreamed he would meet him in a place like this. He licked his lips where he hid in the leafy branches. His heart wouldn't stop pounding. It was like the blood flowing through his body had turned into cheap liquor.

He had once been a Konoha shinobi. Until the Sixth Hokage had dismissed him.

After being exiled from the Land of Fire and moving from group to group as a rogue shinobi, he had at last fallen so low that he had taken a job for this tiny isolated kingdom. But it seemed that his luck had finally turned.

I am going to kill that man today and get my revenge.

He was a Lightning Style user. He'd put on a little show the previous day with the prestigious Lightning Blade because the prime minister had been there, but his specialty was imbuing a shuriken with chakra, transforming that into an electrical current, and hacking an opponent to pieces from a blind spot.

The man held his breath and waited for an opening with Kakashi.

Twelve shinobi surrounded the former Hokage. Some held swords, others readied shuriken, while others watched for a chance to weave signs. Still another held his sheathed sword in a reverse grip and turned the scabbard toward Kakashi, ready for attack.

For a few seconds, it was a stand-off.

The first to move was Kakashi. Without giving his enemy half a second to toss a shuriken, he danced in close and caught the man's chin with the heel of his palm.

In the trees, the man nodded. He would expect nothing less from Kakashi than the nerve to make the first move when surrounded by twelve people.

A heartbeat later, the master ninja dodged the sheath that flew at him, like he had eyes on the back of his head. Looking over his shoulder, he deflected the wrist of a man bringing a sword down on him, and then, suddenly, he looked back at the man hiding in the branches.

He was sure their eyes met.

Instantly, the inside of his body shrank back like a heavy rock had been set in his stomach.

Kakashi quickly averted his eyes and sank down in a fluid motion, dodging the Lightning Style attack that came from behind. And then he looked at the man again.

Those eyes.

The man firmed up his trembling hands. Exactly what did one have to witness and know to end up with eyes like the intruder's? He felt like the hard light in those eyes alone could chop his body to pieces.

Within one heartbeat, the twelve shinobi had all been knocked to the ground.

The man gave up on a surprise attack, climbed down from the tree where he'd been hiding, and revealed himself to Kakashi.

He was a dozen yards away. He leaped sideways to close the distance and got as close as eight yards. He thought that Kakashi had been stabbed dozens of times already, but when he saw him up close, he realized that it was all blood splatter from the other shinobi.

"Shin Hakubi, hm?"

The man lifted his face with a gasp, yanked out of his thoughts about whether to get closer or jump back.

The Lord Hokage actually remembered the face of the man who'd been nothing more than a special jonin. There wasn't a day when the jonin forgot Kakashi's face.

"Hakubi. Is it a coincidence that you're here?"

"Not so sure. Maybe I slipped in to get revenge on the Lord Hokage—" He cut himself off. Kakashi was chuckling for some reason. Feeling like he was being disrespected, he snapped, "I'll make you a dead man right here and now."

He had come to understand something after watching the fighting. Kakashi wasn't using ninjutsu. He probably had almost no chakra left after maintaining that Mud Wall for so long. Most of the shinobi had assumed that the wall was a joint project among several people, but if the master of that technique had been the Sixth Hokage, then it was a different story.

"Heh!" Laughter arose in him. This was the greatest fortune of his life, going one-on-one with the Hokage when he'd used up his chakra.

In his hands, eight shuriken crackled, imbued with electricity.

"I've heard the rumors. You don't have the Sharingan anymore. Haven't for a long time. I don't know why you're still hiding one eye...but you better hope you can follow my Raijin shuriken with the regular eyes you were born with."

He launched the eight shuriken. And another eight at the spot where Kakashi landed after nimbly leaping up to dodge the attack. A heartbeat later, he tossed another eight. The razor-sharp electrical current became one with the shuriken blades, targeting Kakashi from all directions.

No matter which way he ran, one of those spinning stars would hit him. Hakubi would be glad just to get a few blows in. He was under no delusion that he would be able to defeat *the* Hatake Kakashi with a single blow. But he was full of chakra. He would rack up bits of damage slowly and make a sport of killing him, like chasing after a wounded animal.

Kakashi whirled around and dodged the attacks so swiftly, he was almost a blur. He practically flowed past the shuriken. But there were already three blades in his blind spot. Hakubi waited with bated breath for the moment when the ninja was cut to pieces.

Kakashi pushed the headband hiding his left eye up to his eyebrows.

"No!" the man gasped.

The revealed eye shone darkly red. Three sinister tomoe floated up in the iris. Kakashi was supposed to have lost this special Uchiha ability, but there it was in his left eye.

Keeen!

Kakashi knocked back the shuriken that should have been in his blind spot, and the blades cut into Hakubi's shoulder. A second later, pain raced through him, but that didn't matter.

Kakashi of the Sharingan was alive and well?

Ridiculous. There was no way. A reliable source had told him that Kakashi had lost the Sharingan.

But he saw my Raijin shuriken and hit them. There's no way he could pull off a trick like without the Sharingan!

Completely shaken, Hakubi's reaction was slowed, and Kakashi leaped toward him, filling his field of vision. The heel of Kakashi's palm drove into Hakubi's side, and he didn't even have time to feel nauseous before he lost consciousness.

"I can't believe they even had a shinobi from Konoha in their mix," Kakashi muttered with disgust, as he hid his left eye beneath his headband and looked down at the fallen man.

Shin Hakubi. He had once been a special jonin in Konohagakure. His skills weren't too bad, but after learning that he had repeatedly robbed civilians while on missions, Kakashi had dismissed him.

It looked like he'd made the right decision. He dug into the man's bag looking for weapons, and a number of jewels and gold pieces that he had apparently nicked from the palace tumbled out. Among them was a large blue gemstone with a silver chain through it.

He tucked the gem away inside his jacket and turned his

gaze toward the artillery camp. The scattered watchfires shone like fireflies.

He had already slipped past forty-nine naked blades. There was one left.

The rogue shinobi had decided in advance that if there were reports of intruders, they would race in one after the other.

But there was one shinobi who did not abide by this decision. He was the first to notice that the Mud Wall had been released and assumed that the peasants of Nagare would be heading toward the artillery camp.

If he took on the intruder, he would simply be one in a crowd, and his great feats would go unnoticed. It would be easier to take on a bunch of untrained peasants.

In his single-minded desire to monopolize all the glory, the man ran like the wind. He sensed the presence of people on the front line of the artillery camp, waving like seaweed. He was sure that it was the peasants foolishly broadcasting their positions as they carried out their clever plan, not knowing how to extinguish their auras.

No one would complain if he killed them. Mere commoners full of themselves. He'd murder them all.

He smiled slightly, just as darkness fell.

The tip of a bloodstained kunai grazed his face. He threw his head back and just barely avoided having his nose cut off. The intruder? He must have gone around ahead of the man. He kicked at the ground trying to put some distance between them in order to leap away, but someone slammed into his back.

The intruder that had only a millisecond earlier been in front of him was now behind him. He felt a bump on the back of his neck and instantly sleep overcame him.

How can he be that fast...

As he hit the ground, the man heard the intruder say quietly, "That makes fifty..."

•

Nanara and the others managed somehow to slip around to the front of the artillery area, jumping at shadows all the while, expecting to be noticed and shot down at any second.

The light of the torches the guards held flickered here and there at even intervals. Perhaps they had noticed that the wall around the village was gone; the soldiers were starting to run around.

"Nanara, be careful."

"You, too!"

They exchanged farewells in very quiet voices, and Nanara veered even further out of the way, heading to the rear. Meanwhile, the villagers stayed on the front line, so they could pour water on the ammunition powder.

Margo held her breath and groped in the darkness to remove the plug on a cannon. She poured water from her leather bag into the pan and stuck a finger in to check that the powder was wet before running over to the next weapon in line.

They had to water down the pans of as many cannons as possible as quickly as possible. It was only a matter of time before the guards found them. Just when she'd had that thought...

"Ah! You! What are you doing?!"

A guard had found her quickly. The plug she'd removed slipped from her hand with a *klak*.

The guard was unarmed. It seemed that the soldiers had been conscripted to use the large artillery and hadn't been given any personal weapons.

"Listen! I want you to help us." Margo took a chance and started talking to the guard. "You all were conscripted by the prime minister in the capital, right? He made you carry the cannons all this way? It doesn't make sense for you to keep obeying that tyrannical man. Fight together with us."

The man stared hard at her face. "You got any chance of winning?"

"You saw it, didn't you?" she said quickly. "That enormous earth wall? We've got amazing ninja on our side."

"Oh, yeah? Might be worth hearing you out." The man's face softened and he walked toward Margo.

Wonderful. Maybe he'll be an ally.

The moment she let out a sigh of relief, something hit Margo in the face. She reeled and fell, pain dancing along her nerves. As she sat up, she realized that she'd been punched in the face. From beneath the pot on her head, she looked up at the man looking down at her with no expression.

"Why..."

"Sorry, but I can't switch sides," the man said and lit the cannon fuse using the fire of his torch. "My family are being held hostage in the capital. If I go against the prime minister, he'll kill them."

Margo heard a roar behind her, and a projectile shot toward the village of Nagare.

Boom!

The explosion ripped into his ears, and Nanara shuddered.

A cannon had been fired. Which meant that persuading the soldiers wasn't going well.

"I have to hurry...and find my sister."

The rear of the camp was silent. There were no people, only

equipment and provisions. He was sure Manari would be in the safe area to the rear, far from the front lines, and he looked for her there, but he wasn't having any luck.

While he ran around checking each and every tent, the sound of the gunfire grew closer and closer. He appeared to be closing in on the front line to the east.

Boom!

A cannon jetted orange fire on the west side. He could hear the voices of people fighting in the distance. Their little night mission had taken a chaotic turn.

"Nanara!"

Sumure and some adults from the village noticed Nanara and came running over.

"Thank goodness you're all okay," he said with relief.

"For the time being. Anyway, did you find the queen?" Sumure asked.

"No, not yet. My sister and the prime minister are nowhere—" Nanara started, and a hand reached out from behind to grab him.

"If you value the prince's life, don't move!"

Nanara gasped. He'd heard this voice before. It was the man who had roasted and eaten a lizard in the southern district of the capital. So he had been conscripted too.

He struggled to get away, but the hand holding him didn't budge. He almost wondered where this much strength was hiding in such a skinny arm.

The man pressed the blade of a knife to Nanara's throat. "Listen, all of you. If you want him to live, throw down your weapons and water bags before the count of ten. One, two..."

Before he could count to three, there was a clattering sound.

"Sumure, don't be foolish! Pick it up!" Nanara shouted in a rage at Sumure, who had tossed his hoe aside. "There will be

other kings. But if we don't stop the prime minister now, this country will be ruined!"

"Shut up," the man growled and pressed the blade more firmly against the prince's neck.

He felt a pinch as it cut into his skin and then the warmth of dripping blood.

Another hoe fell on top of the one Sumure had thrown aside. Scythes and iron posts clattered to the pile one after another.

Why would you all... Nanara was at a loss for words and bit his lip.

"You all tossed your weapons then? Okay, next, pair up and tie each other's wrists together." The man tossed out the rope coiled at his waist.

Then a mass of brown dropped down into the man's face.

Ray.

Knocking away the knife with his talons, Ray bobbed his head up and down, thrusting his beak at the man's face and head.

"Gah! What is this?!" The man twisted around, and Nanara slipped free of his grip.

The villagers quickly gathered around the man to tie him up with the rope.

"Ray! Thanks!" Nanara called up toward the sky.

As if in response, Ray flew up high and circled in the air.

Following the hawk's movement with his eyes, Nanara's gaze was drawn to one point in particular.

A crimson robe flapped on the cliff to the northeast.

The prime minister. Nanara squinted and saw Manari next to him.

"They were up there..."

To get up to the cliff required a circuitous route over the

pass that went fairly far north from the encampment. Even if he had a horse, it was a half hour's ride from where he stood. But in terms of how the crow flies, it was only three hundred meters. There was no time to lose.

Nanara began to climb the cliff.

Chapter 5

The hand holding the Shuigu was cold with sweat and shaking. Manari stood on the cliff and trembled as she looked down on the battlefield.

Below her, the people of the Land of Redaku were fighting each other.

When the morning sun began to shine, she was able to see much more clearly the state of the encampment blanketed in gunfire smoke. The people fighting all over, pushing and shoving each other.

A soldier who found his chance in the chaos fired in the direction of Nagare. A cannonball grazed the village rooftops and exploded. The blast peeled the roof tiles from the surrounding houses and caused them to collapse as well.

People lived in those houses. Her brother lived in one of them.

She had brought all of this on.

"We were correct to evacuate early, hm?" The prime minister tied his horse to a rocky outcropping and looked down with glee.

Correct? *This* was correct?

She had long stopped being able to follow the prime minister's way of thinking. But she'd never been able to argue with him. She'd simply been dragged along, and now she was here, watching her people fight.

She suddenly remembered the day it was decided that she would inherit the throne. The day the prime minister had handed her this tool. She had been proud to think that she would protect this country, just like her father had.

First, she'd tried to make a light rain fall, enough to wet the vegetation.

She brandished the Shuigu with this intention, but the tool had completely ignored her will. Instead of a gentle shower, it had called up a flash flood. The wheat fields were washed away, mere days from being harvested, and she'd only finally been able to stop the turbulent current when it was on the verge of swallowing the capital. No people had died, but plenty of livestock had been caught in the waters and drowned. It had been a huge blow to the capital's self-sufficiency.

The Shuigu didn't recognize her as ruler. She thought that was why she couldn't use it.

My biggest mistake was becoming queen in the first place.

She felt a belated regret and bit her lip.

Having lost the means of making rain fall, the Land of Redaku was suddenly facing a drought. Some government ministers proposed that she train to use the Shuigu, but Manari had refused. When she thought about how she might destroy the country if it ran wild again, she could not muster up that kind of courage.

This, however, would not resolve the water shortage.

"There is no need to push yourself to try and master it."

The prime minister had been the only one to try and comfort her.

She'd been happy at this kindness, and she trusted the prime minister. Wanting to avert her eyes from the reality before her, she had obediently followed his suggestions.

And this was the result.

His plan was not going well, and it had brought about a civil war.

"My Queen. Be ready to use the Shuigu," the prime minister said.

Manari slowly lifted her face. "But I can't use it."

"There is no need to master it." The prime minister smiled craftily. "We shall simply let it run wild once more and wash away the village in its entirety. A village that won't march in step with its queen is better not existing."

Unable to understand what he was saying, Manari stared at the prime minister. "However dire things are, that's simply..."

"You're saying you can't?" He turned eyes sharp like a hawk on her, and she shrank back.

Timidly, she held the Shuigu up in front of her.

But she quickly lowered her arms.

"I cannot." Murmuring this in a trembling voice was all the resistance she could offer.

The prime minister clucked his tongue and yanked the Shuigu away.

"Give that back!" Manari reached out to take the tool back, but the prime minister sidestepped her and raised the Shuigu.

A massive ball of water flew out and struck her directly in the face. Knocked over by the force of it, Manari fell onto her backside, soaked. A heartbeat later, the mass of water fell over her head with a splash.

"Why..."

The prime minister could clearly handle the Shuigu. Much more skillfully than Manari.

"How...are you able to use the Shuigu?" she asked.

"Hmm. How indeed." The prime minister turned the end of the staff toward Nagare. And then he noticed someone on the cliff wall and snorted with laughter. "Oh my. Your little brother is climbing up the cliff with such vigor."

"Nanara?"

The prime minister brandished the Shuigu, and a current of water began to swirl around the ring at the tip. Just like iron sand gathered around a magnet, the water gradually increased in volume, becoming an enormous sphere.

"Stop!" Manari started to run over to him, but her feet slipped on the wet rock and she fell.

The prime minister brought the Shuigu down.

The stream of water raised its head like an ocean serpent and plunged toward the bottom of the cliff.

Nanara climbed, desperately. The amphiboles that composed the cliff broke easily, making them useful stone material for paving roads, but rendering them a serious hindrance at the moment.

"Ah!" The rock beneath his foot broke away, and he very nearly lost his balance.

He followed the falling stone with his eyes and swallowed hard. He felt like he'd gotten pretty high, but Manari and the prime minister were still far above.

"I have to hurry."

As if to spur him on, the sound of explosions came unceasingly from the ground.

He reached a hand that was already covered in scratches up to a rock above his head. A throb of pain ran through his fingers, but he gritted his teeth to endure it, bent his arm, and pulled his body up.

Then the entire cliff shuddered.

"Hm?"

When he looked up, an enormous body of water was swirling on the edge of the rock face above. It grew in thickness before his eyes to become a torrent and plummet toward him.

"Wha—!" Clutching the cliff, Nanara had nowhere to run. He curled into himself and clenched his jaw.

Just as he was prepared to be swallowed up by water at any second, a hot wind blew past above his head.

"Huh?"

It was an enormous bird of fire. Flaming wings spread, it charged into the center of the oncoming current.

The two slammed into each other, and the powerful heat of the flames lapped up the liquid. The enormous body of water evaporated into mist and disappeared.

Nanara knew this technique. He had pretended to do it over and over and over playing with Sumure in the field.

If Lightning Blade had the power to cut lightning, then this phoenix had enough power to change water into mist. Fire Style Mist. This was one of the Sixth Hokage's many techniques and Nanara's personal favorite.

"You're not hurt?"

He heard a familiar, kind, low voice from directly beside him.

He jerked his head in that direction and found Kakashi standing comfortably on one leg on a foothold the size of a coin.

"Did you...do that? Why would you know the Sixth Hokage's—"

"I'll explain later."

Kakashi held Nanara to one side and nimbly jumped up from rock to rock until he finally flew up unpleasantly high and landed in front of Manari and the prime minister.

The prime minister was not surprised, but instead

narrowed his eyes in a smile. "Well, well, the master tutor! The fact that you're wearing that headband... I knew it. You *are* a shinobi."

Nanara noticed for the first time the headband that covered Kakashi's left eye. A belt of fabric with a board on it. In the center of the board, there were marks where the surface had been carved out.

Why...is he deliberately hiding his left eye? he wondered, while Kakashi leaped to one side, still holding the young prince, to get some distance from the prime minister.

"Hmph. Planning to flee?" Reacting with a quickness that belied his age, the prime minister swung the Shuigu. The pillar of water that jetted out headed straight for Kakashi.

Kakashi set Nanara down on the ground and wove signs. A massive blaze burned above his head, and a phoenix—Mist—came flying out.

Mist stopped in front of Kakashi to protect him and met the pillar of water head on. It wrapped its burning wings around the entire column, swallowed it up, and turned it to vapor.

"Incredible..." the prime minister murmured, entranced, as he stared at the dissipating steam. Of the five styles, Fire should have been weak to Water, but Kakashi's Mist had such power that it turned this disadvantage around to resist the Shuigu. Even though the source of the Shuigu's power was the chakra of the Sage of Six Paths.

"So, Lord Tutor, you were the one who created the earth wall. But after maintaining something like that for over a day, you must have very little chakra remaining?"

"That's what you hope. But I have a quick question for you." Kakashi was unable to hide his anger at the sinister delight in the prime minister's eyes as he asked, "Why can you use the Shuigu when you're not a member of the royal family?"

The instrument in question readied before him, the prime minister said nothing.

Kakashi glanced at the sky before returning his gaze to the older man and asking another question. "Prime minister, so you... You made a contract with the Shuigu before Queen Manari, hm?"

"Contract? What do you mean?" Nanara interjected from behind Kakashi.

"To use a tool imbued with chakra, you generally need a contract between the tool and the user," Kakashi replied. "Most likely, after the king's death, the prime minister secretly made a contract with the Shuigu before the queen."

He turned his gaze toward Manari, who had sunk to the ground and was watching them fight.

"The fact that you can't use the Shuigu isn't your fault. It's just that you don't have a contract with it."

The thoroughly terrified Manari digested Kakashi's words slowly, and a stunned look came across her face.

"Hatake Kakashi. It is just as you say," the prime minister said, laughter in his voice, as he geared up to strike. "I made a contract with the Shuigu before Queen Manari could. ...I am not the king, but I can use the Shuigu. Isn't this fact itself proof that the king is nothing more than decoration?"

"You're going to take her place?" Kakashi asked.

"Exactly!" he shouted and flapped his long sleeves. The ring of the raised Shuigu turned toward Manari.

"Manari! Run!"

Before Nanara had finished shouting, Kakashi had already woven his signs.

Light came from the Shuigu ring, and a whirlpool of water several times larger than the last one began rotating counterclockwise, heading straight for Manari.

At the same time, red-hot embers jumped up on Kakashi's palm. In the blink of an eye, they took on the form of an enormous bird and set out for the whirlpool at the speed of light.

The whirlpool and the bird of flames collided.

Mist's bird shape collapsed, and it returned to being a pile of hot embers, while the whirlpool was thrown back like a curtain from the shock of the collision.

It might have looked like Mist disappeared, but the flames stretched up, licking at the sky, and swallowed the raging stream of water.

Shfff... Both water and fire were cancelled out, and only steam rose into the sky.

"I cannot understand why a shinobi of your caliber would protect an incompetent child," the prime minister sniffed.

"That's a terrible thing to say about the royal family you've served for so many years," Kakashi said.

"I served the previous king!" the prime minister cried, in his hoarse elderly voice. "I swore my loyalty to the previous king, and I served him for more than thirty years. I had no family, I devoted myself to my duties, I wore myself to the bone for this country. And despite this, it was not I who was to be the next king, but you children. Is that not absurd?!"

He glared at Manari and Nanara in turn, eyes burning with anger.

"Is blood so important as that? More than hard work? More than experience?!"

"It's not," Nanara answered in a choked voice. "I know that. The royal family's a sham. We're just regular people. But I've changed since I met Kakashi. Exactly because it is a sham, I want to be the kind of person who's judged by his actions. That's what I've started thinking. So that I can be proud of the blood I inherited from my father."

"If that's what you think, then I will have you die here for your country."

A whirlpool began to swirl at the tip of the Shuigu.

"I've gotten quite good with this instrument, you see. I can also do this." The prime minister smiled and slid the ring to the side. The silhouette of the water bent and transformed into a massive bird.

As if in response, flames jetted above Kakashi's head and manifested a burning Mist.

Bird of flames versus bird of water. The one that took the initiative was the bird of water. It had no sooner stretched out its long neck than it was letting out a roar and vomiting a column of water. To meet this, the bird of flames spat out a pillar of flame.

Water and fire crashed into each other violently.

But in the next instant, fire pushed water back. The flames swallowed up the column of water and kept pushing forward to pierce the body of the bird. The creature let out a death cry as it emitted scalding hot steam and disappeared.

With this fourth summoning of Mist, Kakashi had basically used up all his chakra, but he called to the prime minister with a casual look to keep him from sensing this fact.

"Say. If you defeat me here and invade the Land of Fire, that group of shinobi you've assembled don't have a chance of winning. I mean, you have to know that, right?"

"Hmph," the prime minister snorted. "I told you that we would be receiving support from the astronomical institute. I was never counting on the cannons or the shinobi army alone. Not to mention I have the Shuigu. This tool that allows me to use the chakra of the Sage of Six Paths, the father of all shinobi, and as long as I—"

"It is not a weapon for killing people!" Nanara cried, trembling with anger. "It's... It's to bring water to this country. It's your fault that people are starving in the capital. You took the Shuigu from my sister and made a mess of the land!"

Boom.

He heard a cannon fire far below them. While they were standing around up here, Nagare was under attack. The faces of Margo, Sumure, and all the villagers popped into his head one after the other, and Nanara twisted his own face up.

"A small sacrifice for a great cause," the prime minister spat, annoyed that the prince could not understand this. "The reason this country is poor is the land. Unable to trade in any real way with other countries, we content ourselves with the limited crops we can take from these barren lands and shut ourselves away to live in secret. No matter how much time passes, we do not develop. I want to make the Land of Redaku like the Land of Fire! I will turn this backward nation, where people die simply because it does not rain, into an advanced country that controls nature with powerful technology. To that end, we need new, fertile land."

He shifted his gaze from Nanara to Kakashi.

"Shinobi of the Land of Fire. Born and raised in wealth, you would force us to live in poverty in the middle of nowhere?"

There was a brief silence.

Kakashi looked past the older man toward the sky spreading out behind him.

"Prime Minister. It's all fine and good to look to other countries, but you're holding onto phantoms here. It's not like the Land of Fire has always been rich. We had a period of stagnation and ruin, full of endless war with no purpose."

Kakashi took the glove off his right hand and tossed it aside.

"A country that went through war and became rich, and a country that has lived quietly avoiding war—I don't know which way is better. But at the very least, this place was at peace until the previous king's generation. And now you're planning to invade my homeland. As a shinobi of Konoha, I can't let that pass."

"We are not going to see eye to eye, hm?" The prime minister caressed the staff of the Shuigu and smiled. "A practitioner like you, I would have loved to have you with me. It's too bad. Shall we stop this idle argument here then?"

"Mm, agreed. Nothing more boring than a long story from an old man," Kakashi quipped, and the prime minister's gaze grew even harder.

But his expression froze when Kakashi slowly removed the headband that hid his left eye.

"That eye," he gasped.

Kakashi's left eye shone faintly, imbued with a red light and patterned with tomoe. Anyone who had more than a passing knowledge of shinobi would have heard about it from someone. The proud name Kakashi of the Sharingan blasted through every country.

"I see." The prime minister's lips twisted up into a grin. "You are Kakashi of the Sharingan then?"

His tone was casual, but the old hand that gripped the Shuigu trembled slightly. It seemed that he truly did feel fear knowing that a shinobi of great legend stood before him.

"I heard that Hatake Kakashi lost his Sharingan in the Great Ninja War some dozen years ago. A false rumor then?"

"Mm." Kakashi shrugged. "Sadly, it's just as you see. My Sharingan is alive and well."

"Hmph. No matter what talents you have, you don't begin to compare to the Sage of Six Paths' power," the prime minister spat.

"How pathetic."

The prime minister froze and glared at the ninja. "What did you say?"

"You're mistaking for your own strength the power of a tool you just happened to get hold of. But that misunderstanding won't last long."

Kakashi glanced up at the sky again. The cloud of evaporation generated in the collision between Mist and the Shuigu had been knocked away by the wind from below and was rolling up high into the sky.

"The mist has cleared away," he said. "Your future is death."

"You brat! Don't be so full of yourself!" The prime minister raised the Shuigu up above his head.

Abruptly, there was an incredible clap of thunder, and a burst of lightning struck the prime minister.

Illuminated by the white bolt, the area was nothing but light and shadow for a few seconds.

The prime minister fell to his knees, where the rock had broken away to form a deep fissure.

"What...happened..." Eyes and ears spinning from the sudden roar and impact, Nanara collapsed on the spot and gaped upward.

Even though the dawn in the eastern sky was without a cloud, a grey mass hung above Nanara's head.

The massive amount of steam generated by the battle between Kakashi and the prime minister had turned into a cumulonimbus cloud in the rising air currents because of Mist's heat, causing friction with the cold air in the area and leading to a thundercloud. The Shuigu the prime minister brandished became a lightning rod and called down the strike. The bolt became a hundred million volts of divine punishment to pierce the prime minister's body.

Pop!

Hidden by the cloud of sand that danced up in the lightning strike, Kakashi released his transformation technique.

There was no change in his appearance. Well, almost none; the tomoe of the Sharingan in his eye had disappeared.

With transformation jutsu, he could make it look like he had the Sharingan. It was a cheap trick, but thanks to how well

known the name Kakashi of the Sharingan was, it ended up being a fairly effective bluff to avoid pointless fighting. When he used it together with a smoke bomb with genjutsu effects, most shinobi got the wrong idea: that Kakashi of the Sharingan still existed and was doing just fine.

At some point, the sound of gunfire from below the cliff had stopped. The prime minister toppled into the fissure in the stone face. Kakashi ran over, sat him up, and ripped open his gown to find a lightning pattern rising clearly on his flat chest.

"Kakashi! That lightning—"

"I'll explain later." He quickly cut off Nanara and put an ear to the old man's chest. When he confirmed that his heart had stopped, he brought his glove-free hand down and began to push on the center of his chest.

Belatedly realizing that Kakashi was doing CPR, Nanara went around to the prime minister's head and made sure his airway was clear. When Kakashi stopped pushing on his chest, Nanara put his mouth over the prime minister's and blew air in.

But they got no reaction, although they continued to do the chest compressions for a while.

Just as Nanara was starting to think that it was too late, the prime minister spat up blood.

"What a relief... He came back..." Nanara checked that the man was indeed breathing again, and then all the strength ran out of his body. He dropped to the ground. His limbs suddenly felt very heavy.

So many things had happened these last few days, and he was incredibly tired.

Kakashi really was an amazing guy. He always stayed calm, whatever the situation, and guided Nanara forward. There probably wasn't another guy as reliable as him.

Lying on his back and looking up at the sky, Nanara heard Kakashi's hoarse voice.

"Aah, good..."

His eyes grew wide. He had overheard what was probably Kakashi speaking to himself unconsciously.

Was it the prime minister's resuscitation that was "good"? Was it that they won the fight? Or that they were able to get the Shuigu back? Whatever it was, Kakashi had just barely managed it.

Nanara sat up slowly and looked at his tutor, whose face was damp with sweat. It was hard to tell because of the mask, but when he looked closely, Kakashi was terribly pale.

His constant composure was a bluff. He had just been pretending he was fine. The truth was, he was struggling.

Nanara wondered whether he should go and hold Kakashi up but quickly gave up on the idea.

He had probably always lived like this. Hiding his feelings, chipping away at himself, he had fought with a level head and a cool look. Always to protect someone.

Nanara prayed that he hadn't always lived this life alone. He had no idea if this were true, but he felt sure Kakashi had been blessed with amazing friends, and he'd been able to keep fighting all this time because he had people supporting him. He wanted that to be true.

Otherwise, it was just too painful.

Even after being struck by lightning, the Shuigu didn't have a scratch on it. Kakashi examined it and found that the ring on the end could come off. He pulled out a small scroll from inside the staff.

"Kakashi, that's..." Nanara started.

"The Shuigu contract, I suppose." That would explain why Kakashi hadn't been able to find it no matter how he'd searched the office.

He spread the scroll out. Just like with a summoning contract, the previous king's name and fingerprint were on it in blood. Immediately to the left of this was the prime minister's name.

"Nanara. You make the contract," Manari said decisively. "I ended up the prime minister's puppet and made a mess of the country. I should be punished together with him."

Nanara looked at the Shuigu in Kakashi's hand and fell silent. Even though he'd made up his mind to become king, his resolve wavered before his older sister.

"It's okay," she told him. "I'm sure you will become a great leader. Just like the Sixth Hokage."

That last bit gave him the push he needed. He scrunched up his face and looked at Kakashi. "I want to make the contract. What should I do?"

Kakashi cut the tip of Nanara's finger with a knife and made him sign his name. Only a short while ago, he hadn't been able to write the name he signed now. After he pressed his fingertip on the page below it, he looked up with an anxious face.

"I did it. What do I do now?"

"That's it," Kakashi said. "Now you should be able to use the Shuigu."

A doubtful look on his face, Nanara gripped the staff. Even though it was the first time he'd touched it, it fit neatly into his hand.

This tool was, for Nanara, a present from three fathers. One was the Sage of Six Paths, who had brought water to this dry land and helped his ancestors to build the country. The second was his actual father, who had ruled this country wisely and passed on the tool to Nanara's generation. And the third was, of course...

"Can you use it?" Manari peered at him anxiously.

Nanara nodded firmly. "It's good. I can tell."

He stood on the edge of the cliff and held the Shuigu up high.

The decorative bit hanging from the ring made a clear ringing sound and began to shake. He felt something like an invisible force pour out of the Shuigu. Was it chakra? The special power that the Sage of Six Paths had left for them so long ago, a prayer that this country would prosper.

The chakra slowly spread out, like the ripples made by a leaf on the surface of water. Eventually, droplets hit his cheeks.

"Rain..." Manari murmured, holding out the palm of her hand.

The long-awaited rain began to gently moisten the earth.

The water soaked into the dry ground.

A wet Kakashi looked at Nanara holding up the Shuigu. He would lead the country from now on as its young king. Kakashi knew in his bones just how difficult a job it was to walk ahead of others as their leader. It wasn't an easy road, but he was sure Nanara could make it.

Sometimes, he wasn't sure if the things he had done as Hokage had been right.

Sudden developments were accompanied by significant pain. While Kakashi had given birth to something new when he changed society, a lot of things had disappeared. The minority was sometimes cut away for the sake of the majority.

When he did meet Obito again someday, would he be able to hold his head high? Be confident that he had properly fulfilled his duties as the Sixth Hokage?

The one who had given him the answer to these questions without the slightest hesitation had been an unschooled boy who couldn't read.

The Sixth Hokage is the most powerful shinobi! And the greatest leader!

That was the only time he'd been happy from the bottom of his heart that he hid his face behind a mask. To think his cheeks could get that hot at a few words from a child he'd only just met.

•

It was decided that the prime minister would be returned to the capital and tried under the laws of the land. The rogue shinobi would also be returned to their respective villages.

The rain Nanara had made fall dampened the ammunition powder and rendered the cannons useless. The fighting ended, and the people finally came together to rejoice in the blessing of the rain, no longer enemy or ally.

The village buildings had been destroyed, but the people who had evacuated were all safe. And while a great number of people had been injured in the fighting in the artillery camp, there had been no deaths.

"None of us had any real weapons, after all. And the village was empty," the grown-ups said with bitter smiles. But the fact that no one had died was better proof than anything that no one had truly wanted this war.

After waiting for the rain to end, Nanara gathered everyone in the plaza and announced his sister's retirement.

"So that means you're the king now, Nanara?" Margo asked.

"Well...I guess it kind of does..." Nanara replied, embarrassed.

The villagers surrounded him, grinning.

"Nanara, you have to say a little something. Now that you're king, you have to give speeches all the time."

"That'll be after the formal coronation in the capital," he protested.

"Come on, practice now."

"No, it's embarrassing," he said and tried to escape, but the grown-ups caught him.

"You're the king," Margo said. "You can't be embarrassed by people like us."

He realized that she was right and gave up the fight. He climbed onto a bale of hay and stood tall, his hands thrust into the pockets of his jacket.

"Hey! That's pretty rude! The king can't be sticking his hands in his pockets!" Sumure jeered and nipped his grand moment in the bud.

"Shut up! This is fine!"

He couldn't exactly display his hands to everyone when they were covered in cuts from climbing the cliff. Nanara had learned from Kakashi that enduring the pain and walking ahead of people was the role of a leader.

He looked down at the villagers from his bale of hay and began to speak, looking at each of their faces in turn. What he wanted to do as king. What he *had* to do. He was still young and inexperienced, and there were so many things he didn't know. He hoped they would all help him.

He wasn't very good at explaining difficult things, so he got stuck on the words, despite how certain his feelings were. When he felt the panic rising up in him, he looked out at Kakashi standing all the way at the back and was able to relax.

He had so many questions. But Kakashi just kept repeating, "I'll explain later." Nanara had to interrogate him as soon as this speech was over!

The thing he most wanted to ask was: Who exactly *are* you? And well, he had an idea about that, but he would make Kakashi tell him himself. And then he would get angry that Kakashi had kept it a secret all this time, and then he'd thank him for helping him...

When he met Kakashi's eyes, Kakashi smiled, the corners of his eyes wrinkling.

Even though he was in the middle of a speech, Nanara also smiled finally, unconsciously.

That was the last time he saw Kakashi.

After his speech, he ran all over in search of him, but Kakashi was nowhere to be found. All that he left behind was the blue gem that was a keepsake of Nanara's father, tucked into the pocket of Nanara's coat.

Final Chapter

Six months after Hatake Kakashi vanished from the Land of Redaku, the new king, Nanara, was seeing his first winter after inheriting the throne. Soon, the mountains would be covered in snow, and people from neighboring villages would no longer be able to come and go until spring came.

That fall there had been an unprecedented harvest. The rainfall the king made filled rivers and brought water to the fields, and the wheat crops thrived. All the villages had enough food and feed to make it through the winter.

"Nanara, there's a letter from Konohagakure." Manari came into the office with Ray in tow.

After stepping down from the throne, Manari had wanted to be punished in the same way as the prime minister. But she had yielded to the firm request of the government officials and been appointed an internal aide. She took on the paperwork that Nanara was bad at doing himself and helped Nanara however he needed to restore the country.

Ray flew up from her arm and landed on the perch on Nanara's desk. He made chirping sounds as if seeking praise for

making his long trip to and from the Land of Fire. In his talons was a small package.

A present from the Seventh Hokage, Uzumaki Naruto. He opened it: a book. On the cover, it said, "All-Ages Version: The New Make-Out Paradise."

"Oh! This is the book that Kakashi was talking about!" Nanara picked it up and giggled.

A thick, deluxe edition wrapped in a shiny jacket. Next to the promotional blurb on the bottom that said "Recommended by the Sixth Hokage!" was a photo of the Sixth Hokage holding up a thumb and winking. He had bleary, sleepy eyes, a somehow absentminded man.

How dare he not say a thing all this time!

As if reading Nanara's mind, Ray gave a short cry and shook his head.

It's better to avoid a fight than win it. When had Kakashi said that? A good leader didn't win battles, they prevented one from even starting. If that were true, then Kakashi really was the best leader.

Stroking the cover of *All-Ages Version: The New Make-Out Paradise*, Nanara suddenly felt like crying and hurried to compose himself.

His encounter with Kakashi was the best present connecting him with the previous king.

•

Fifteen days after saving the Land of Redaku and leaving Nanara, Kakashi returned to the village of Konohagakure. The journey that had taken twenty days was slightly shorter on the return, now that he knew the roads.

The first place he headed was a bar in the new city. A server

who knew him smiled wryly when he saw Kakashi and pointed him to a seat in the back. On the other side of the closed sliding doors, he heard familiar voices screaming in revelry. The party he said that he might be able to attend appeared to be in full swing.

He finally relaxed. The celebratory mood made it easier. His undercover mission to an unknown land was over, and he had made it back to a familiar environment. He was also keenly aware of how precious and rare it was to have comrades who could make him feel this way.

He was late and would be noticed, so he used his honed skills as a ninja to make himself invisible and quietly open the sliding door at one end to mix in with the crowd. At least that was the plan. A brilliant former student from the Foundation who excelled at detecting people got behind him suddenly and clasped his shoulder.

"Honestly! You're so late, Master! I thought you weren't coming!"

It was Sai. He appeared to be pretty drunk; his face was bright red.

"Aah, I just got the start time wrong," Kakashi lied, with a wry smile. Only a few people had been informed of his mission to the Land of Redaku and his purpose there.

"Anyway, Sai, where's your wife?" He casually changed the subject.

"I'm right here!" Ino poked her face out from behind Sai. Her cheeks were slightly flushed, but not nearly to the extent of Sai's. Known for being a handsome couple, the two of them made a pretty picture even if the venue was a bar for the common rabble.

Sai hadn't begun drinking until recently. People in Black Ops couldn't get drunk and lose control, after all. And he turned out to be an absurdly cheap drunk. He'd only started drinking

with people once the country had stabilized and the frequency of being called for an urgent mission dropped dramatically. It was very funny how tipsy he got after drinking the tiniest bit, and everyone would haze him and pour drinks down his throat.

"What are you drinking, Master? The new stuff they got in from the Land of Waves wash yummyyyy!" Sai said and offered not a menu but a bamboo plate of tempura.

Kakashi thanked him and took the plate, handing it to Ino in the same flowing motion as he set himself down in a chair in the corner.

Ino held up an unsteady Sai. When Kiba began to make fun of them and the way they clung to each other, Karui whacked him on the head and told him not to be crude. Next to her, Lee, with glazed-over eyes, turned toward the olive branch decorating the table and began speaking intently. Choji was yelling at Tenten, "Why would you eat all the kara'age chicken by yourself?!"

They're all so full of life...

Kakashi sipped sake as he stared absently out at the festive group. They had long since reached adulthood, and some were now parents while others were active on the front lines as shinobi. Even so, no matter how many years passed, to Kakashi, they were his precious students and the next generation who needed to be protected. Seeing them having so much fun was enough to ease his heart. If Asuma and Hayate had been alive, they no doubt would have thought the same thing.

As Kakashi indulged in an emotional moment, a square glass was thrust forward before him. Amber liquid poured over a large sphere of ice filled the glass.

"Welcome back, Master Kakashi." The current Hokage sat down next to him and clinked glasses.

Downing the spirits dulled the fatigue of returning from a mission, and Kakashi leaned against the sliding door.

"You really helped me out going to the Land of Redaku."
Naruto turned his blue eyes on him. "Whatever the country
might be like, I definitely wanted to avoid a war, and I didn't
want any embers for future fights."

"Be good to the new king," Kakashi replied. "He said he's
going to try and do what he can."

"Of course. He's your student, and I used to be your
student, so we're practically brothers." Naruto's voice was as
forceful and confident as always. But when Kakashi took a peek
at the Hokage's face when he wasn't looking, he couldn't say
his former student looked good, not even to flatter him. The
slight haggardness of his cheeks wasn't just because of the many
demands placed on the Hokage.

We have to do something soon...

Kakashi watched for the right time and left the bar.

A humid breeze blew outside. Perhaps because he was at a
much lower altitude now, the moon and stars felt further away
than when he'd looked up at them in the Land of Redaku.

Shikamaru was leaning against the wall of the bar smoking
a cigarette while he waited for Kakashi. "Master Kakashi. Welcome back from your mission."

"Where are Sakura and Sasuke?"

"They're still not back from the astronomical institute. I
guess things got complicated there."

"Oh yeah?" Kakashi said. "Well, those two should be fine."

"Yes. The issue is with Naruto's illness," Shikamaru said,
lowering his voice and tucking his cigarette butt into a portable
ashtray. He furrowed his brow in annoyance and pulled out a
second cigarette from the case his wife had given him. "If we
don't hurry, we'll run out of time. Naruto will always—"

"Aaaah! It's the Siiiiixth!" came a cheerful voice from the
other side of the road.

Three pairs of annoying footfalls grew closer. Boruto, Sarada, and Mitsuki.

When they heard the children's voices, Kakashi and Shikamaru wiped the serious looks from their faces.

"Oooold maaaaan Kakashiiiii! It's been like forever!"

"What, you kids are here too?" Shikamaru put away the cigarette he had taken out and indicated the curtain over the door curtly. "Everyone's inside. Go on and eat supper or something."

"All right! Someone else is paying!" Boruto threw his arms up in the air.

"Don't take advantage of the chaos and drink alcohol," Shikamaru said sternly. "Kids get juice."

"We *know*!"

"I'm heading out. I got a present for Master Iruka," Sarada said, holding up a cherry pink paper bag. Strawberry daifuku from Tami Traditional Sweets in the old city. They were widely known to be extraordinary and quickly sold out, so they were hard to get ahold of, a rare treat.

"Oh right, you're doing a homestay at Master Iruka's, right?" Kakashi said.

"Yeah!" Sarada nodded happily. "Cuz Mom and Dad are away on a long mission. Master Iruka's an amazing cook. He's teaching me all kinds of stuff. It's loads of fun."

"Ohh. He is pretty skilled."

Iruka was a longtime bachelor like Kakashi, but unlike Kakashi, who paid little attention to his personal life to start with, Iruka kept a neat home. In contrast with the desk of the Sixth Hokage, which was always covered with scattered papers and documents, the principal's office at the academy was famously neat and tidy.

"Sixth, you haven't been in the village at all lately," Mitsuki said. "Where'd you go?"

"Mm. Just visiting some onsens," Kakashi lied without batting an eye. Naturally, even his son Boruto hadn't been told that Naruto was in a difficult situation. Kakashi had promised not to tell.

"Onsens again? Old Man Kakashi, you're aaaalllways at the onsen." Boruto looked at Kakashi, exasperated. "You'll turn into a prune if all you do is sit in the tub, you know."

"Wouldn't like that at all." Kakashi smiled, his sleepy eyes narrowing.

Masashi Kishimoto

Author/artist Masashi Kishimoto was born in 1974 in rural Okayama Prefecture, Japan. After spending time in art college, he won the Hop Step Award for new manga artists with his manga *Karakuri* (Mechanism). Kishimoto decided to base his next story on traditional Japanese culture. His first version of *Naruto*, drawn in 1997, was a one-shot story about fox spirits; his final version, which debuted in *Weekly Shonen Jump* in 1999, quickly became the most popular ninja manga in Japan.

Jun Esaka

Born February 13 in Kanagawa Prefecture.
Blood type O. After graduating from Waseda University,
he began working as a writer.

RELISH MASASHI KISHIMOTO'S ARTWORK IN ALL ITS COLORFUL GLORY

The Art of NARUTO

Complete your *NARUTO* collection with the hardcover art book, *The Art of NARUTO: Uzumaki*, featuring:

- Over 100 pages of full-color *NARUTO* manga images
- Step-by-step details on creating a *NARUTO* illustration
- Notes about each image
- An extensive interview with creator Masashi Kishimoto

Plus, a beautiful double-sided poster!

Available at your local bookstore or comic store

SHONEN JUMP   VIZ

NARUTO

ORIGINAL CONCEPT BY
MASASHI KISHIMOTO

The ninja adventures continue in these stories featuring the characters of **Naruto** and **Boruto**!

SASUKE'S STORY
STAR PUPIL

MASASHI KISHIMOTO
JUN ESAKA

NARUTO'S STORY
FAMILY DAY

SHIKAMARU'S STORY
MOURNING CLOUD

STORY BY
TAKASHI YANO

STORY BY
MIREI MIYAMOTO

STORY BY
JUN ESAKA

A new series of prose novels, straight from the worldwide **Naruto** franchise. Naruto's allies and enemies take center stage in these fast-paced adventures, with each volume focusing on a particular clan mate, ally, team…or villain.

VIZ

BORUTO
=NARUTO NEXT GENERATIONS=

CREATOR/SUPERVISOR **Masashi Kishimoto**
ART BY **Mikio Ikemoto** SCRIPT BY **Ukyo Kodachi**

A NEW GENERATION OF NINJA IS HERE!

Naruto was a young shinobi with an incorrigible
knack for mischief. He achieved his dream to
become the greatest ninja in his village, and
now his face sits atop the Hokage monument.
But this is not his story... A new generation
of ninja is ready to take the stage, led by
Naruto's own son, Boruto!

KAKASHI'S STORY